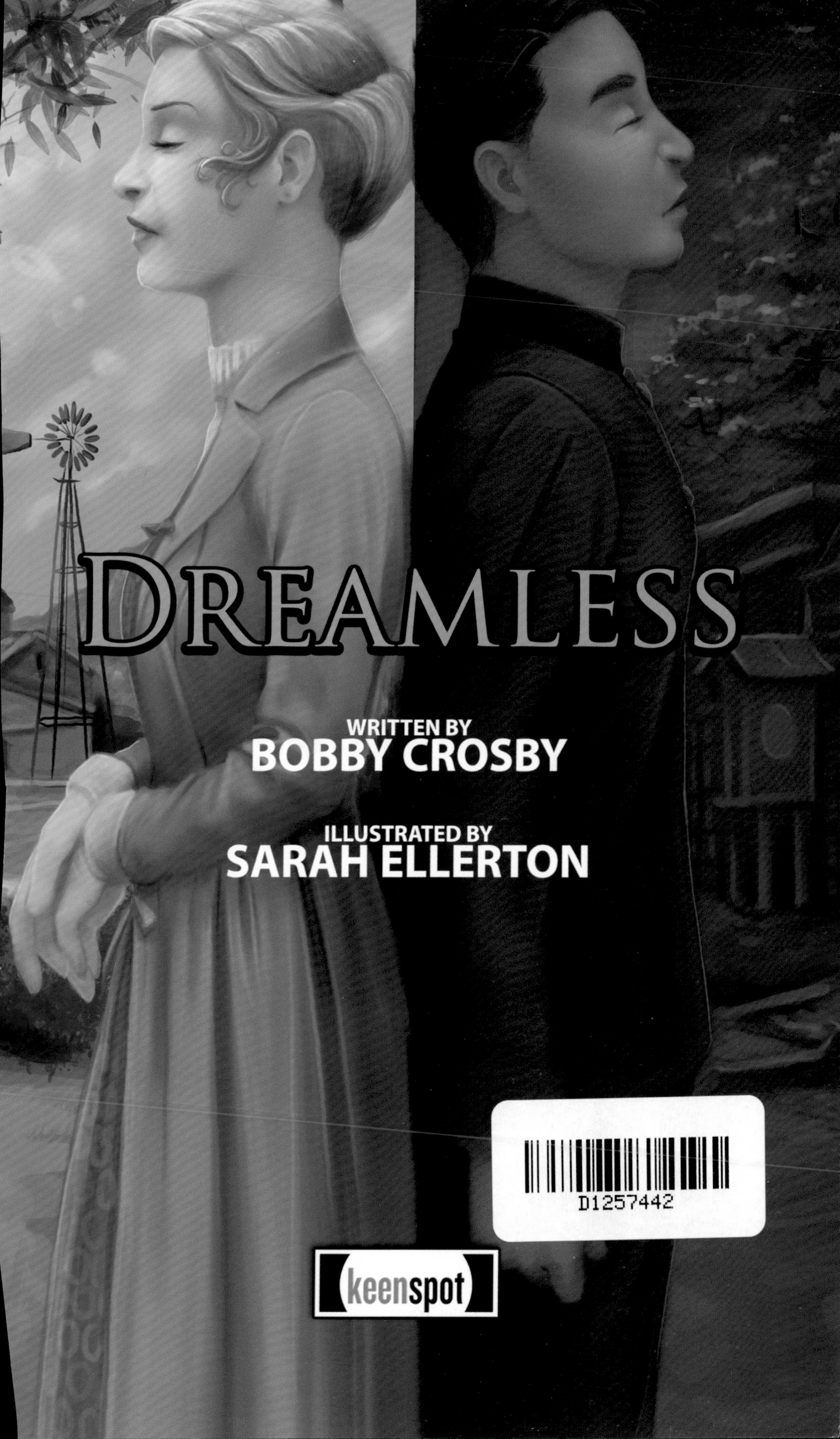
DREAMLESS
WRITTEN BY
BOBBY CROSBY
ILLUSTRATED BY
SARAH ELLERTON
keenspot

DREAMLESS

DREAMLESS and all related characters are © and ™ 2009-2021 by Bobby Crosby.

This book collects material originally published online as serialized webcomics at dreamlessmovie.com beginning in January 2009 and in a printed graphic novel published by Blatant Comics in July 2010.

Published by
Keenspot Entertainment
Apple Valley, CA
E-Mail: keenspot@keenspot.com
Web: www.keenspot.com

For Keenspot
CEO & EiC Chris Crosby
PRESIDENT Bobby Crosby

ISBN 1-932775-74-9
First Keenspot Printing, April 2021
Printed in USA

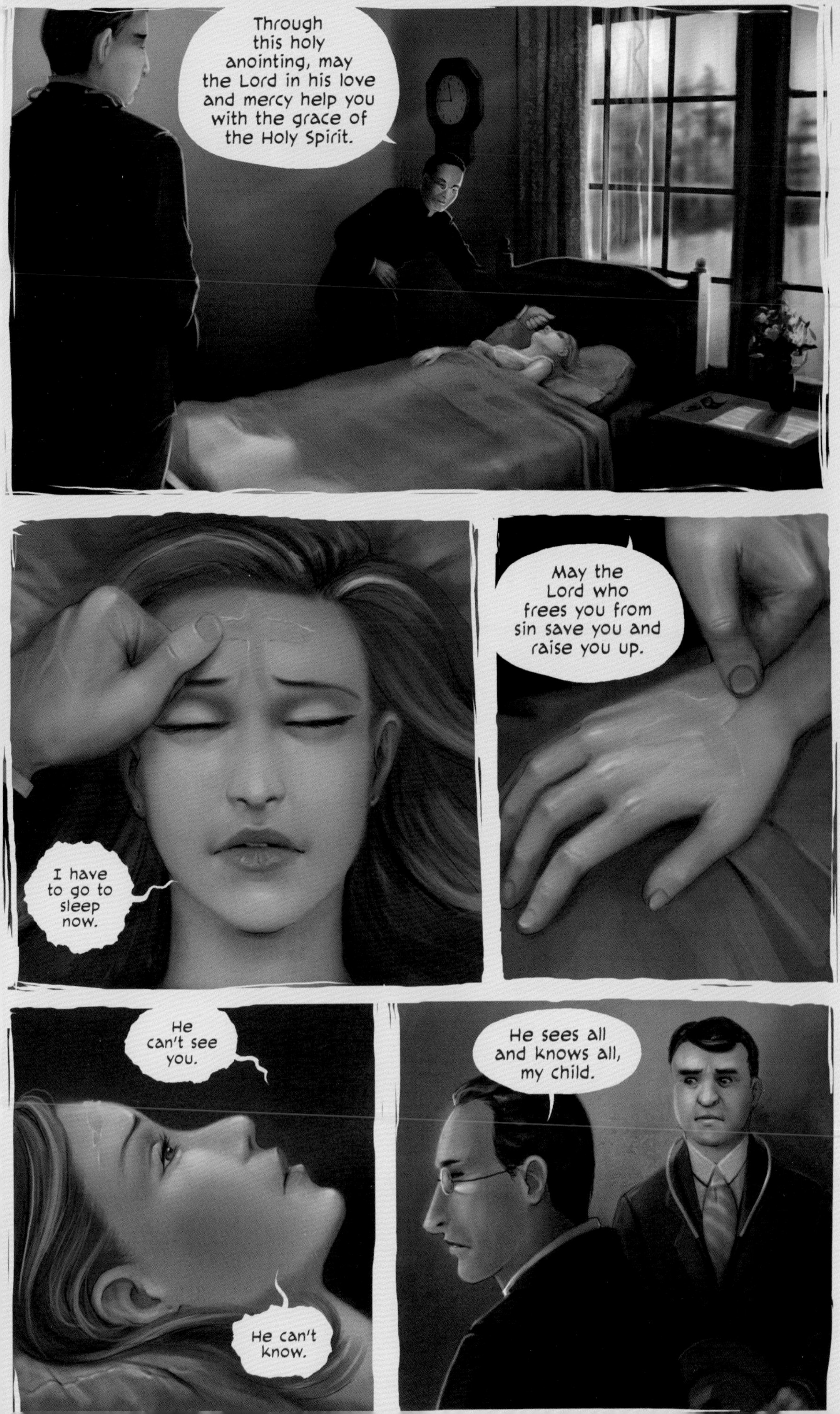
Through this holy anointing, may the Lord in his love and mercy help you with the grace of the Holy Spirit.
I have to go to sleep now.
May the Lord who frees you from sin save you and raise you up.
He can't see you.
He can't know.
He sees all and knows all, my child.

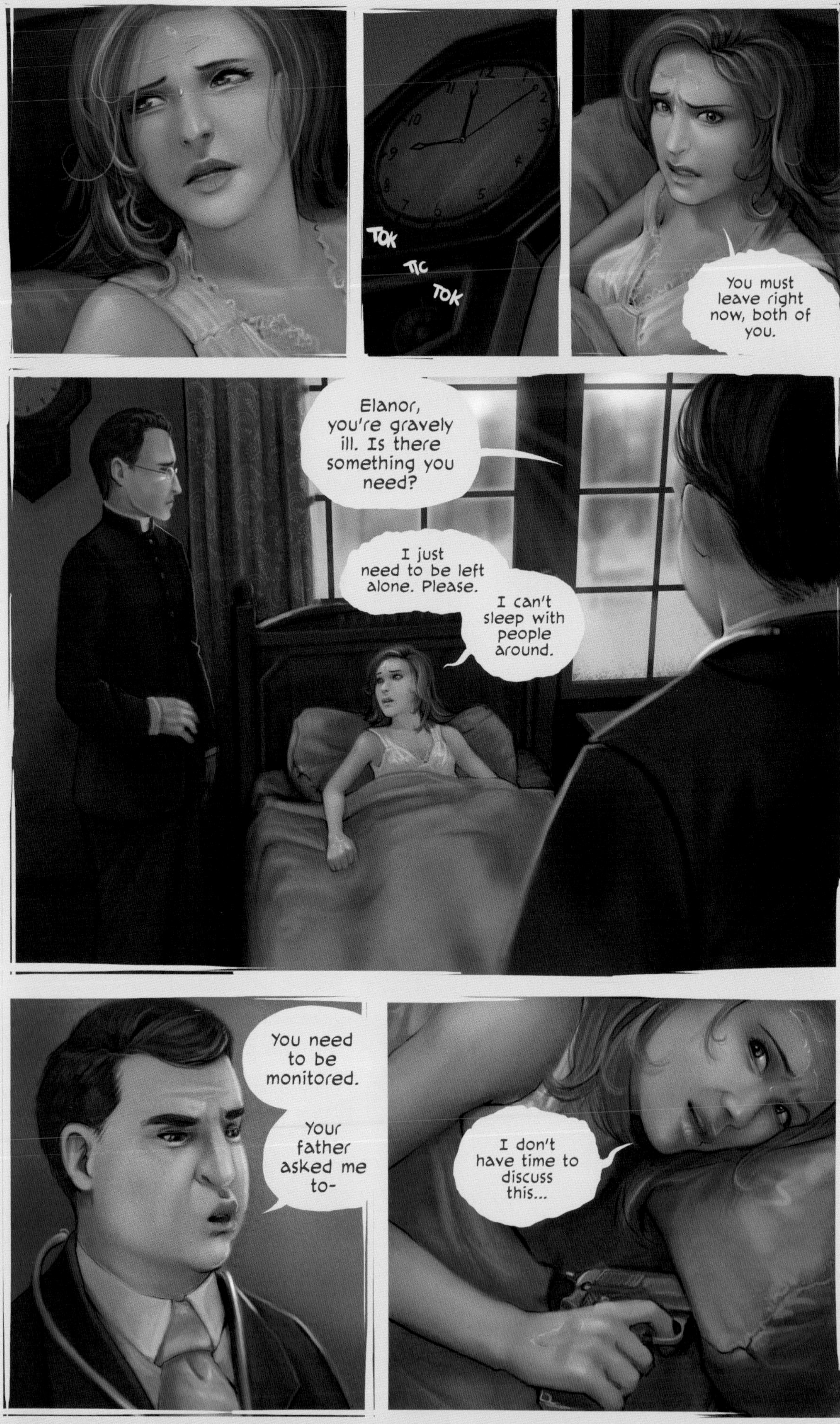
TOK
TIC
TOK
You must leave right now, both of you.
Elanor, you're gravely ill. Is there something you need?
I just need to be left alone. Please.
I can't sleep with people around.
You need to be monitored.
Your father asked me to-
I don't have time to discuss this...

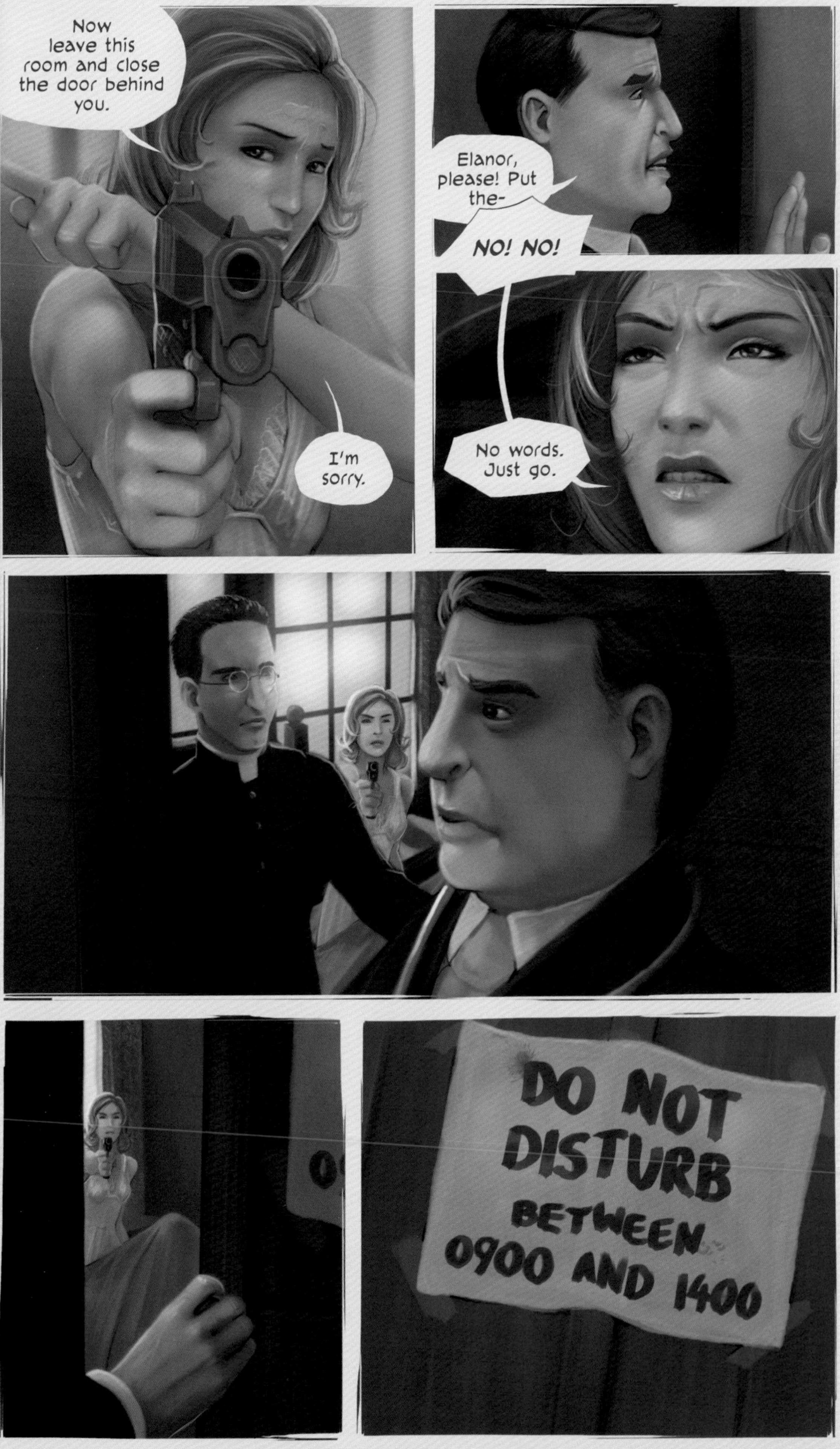
Now leave this room and close the door behind you.
I'm sorry.
Elanor, please! Put the-
NO! NO!
No words. Just go.
DO NOT DISTURB
BETWEEN
0900 AND 1400

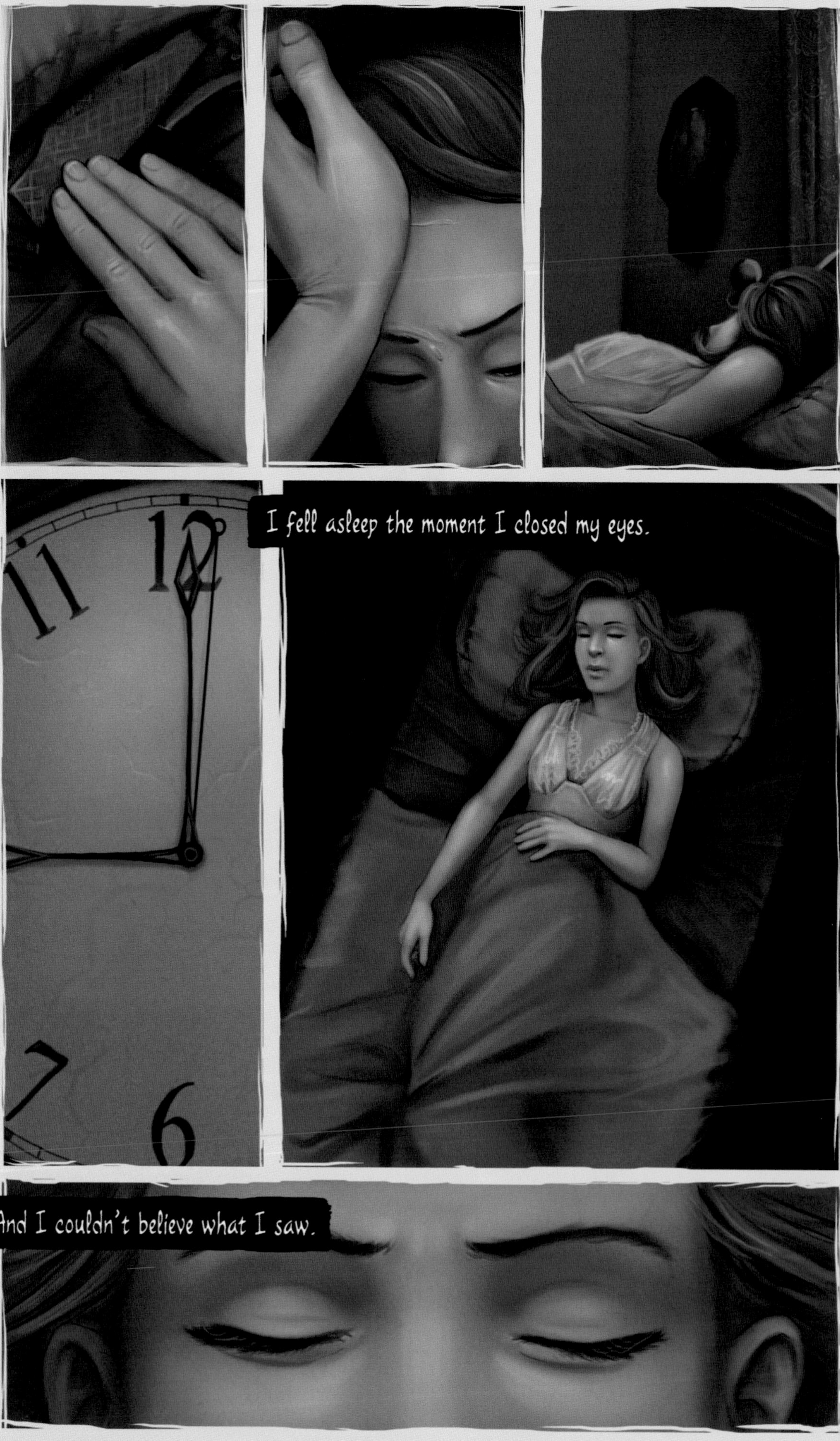
I fell asleep the moment I closed my eyes.
And I couldn't believe what I saw.

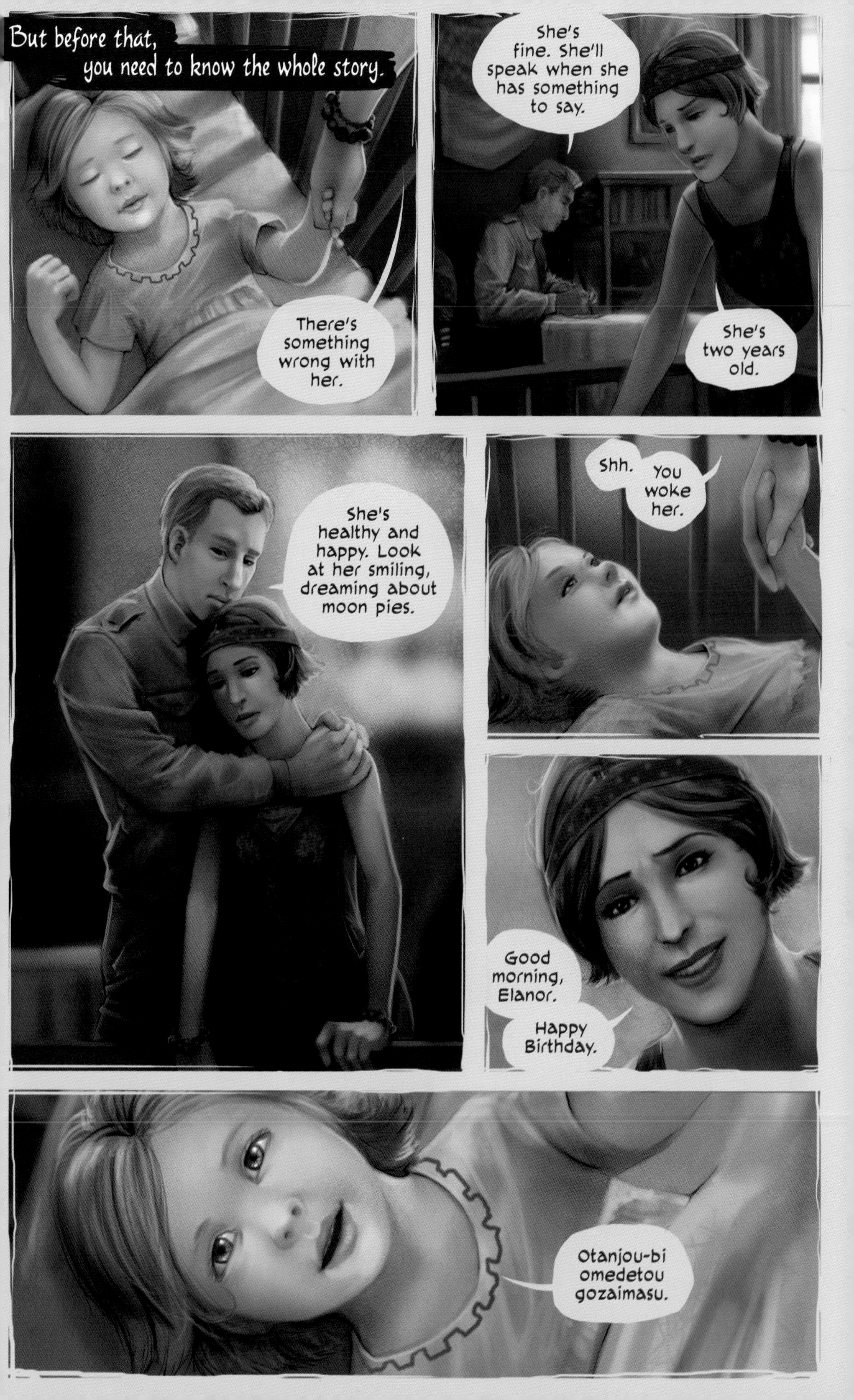

But before that, you need to know the whole story.
There's something wrong with her.
She's fine. She'll speak when she has something to say.
She's two years old.
She's healthy and happy. Look at her smiling, dreaming about moon pies.
Shh.
You woke her.
Good morning, Elanor.
Happy Birthday.
Otanjou-bi omedetou gozaimasu.

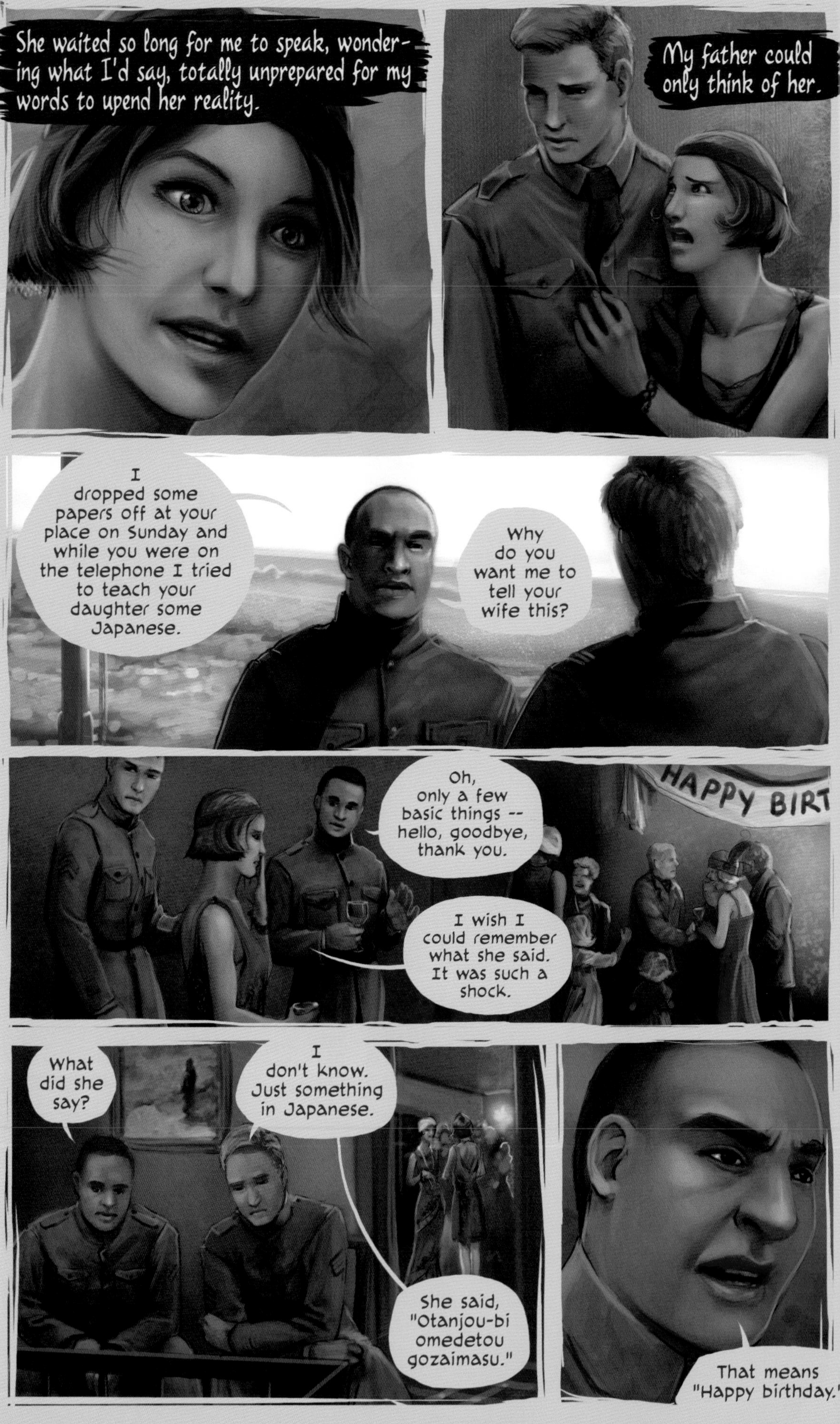
She waited so long for me to speak, wondering what I'd say, totally unprepared for my words to upend her reality.
My father could only think of her.
I dropped some papers off at your place on Sunday and while you were on the telephone I tried to teach your daughter some Japanese.
Why do you want me to tell your wife this?
HAPPY BIRT
Oh, only a few basic things -- hello, goodbye, thank you.
I wish I could remember what she said. It was such a shock.
What did she say?
I don't know. Just something in Japanese.
She said, "Otanjou-bi omedetou gozaimasu."
That means "Happy birthday."

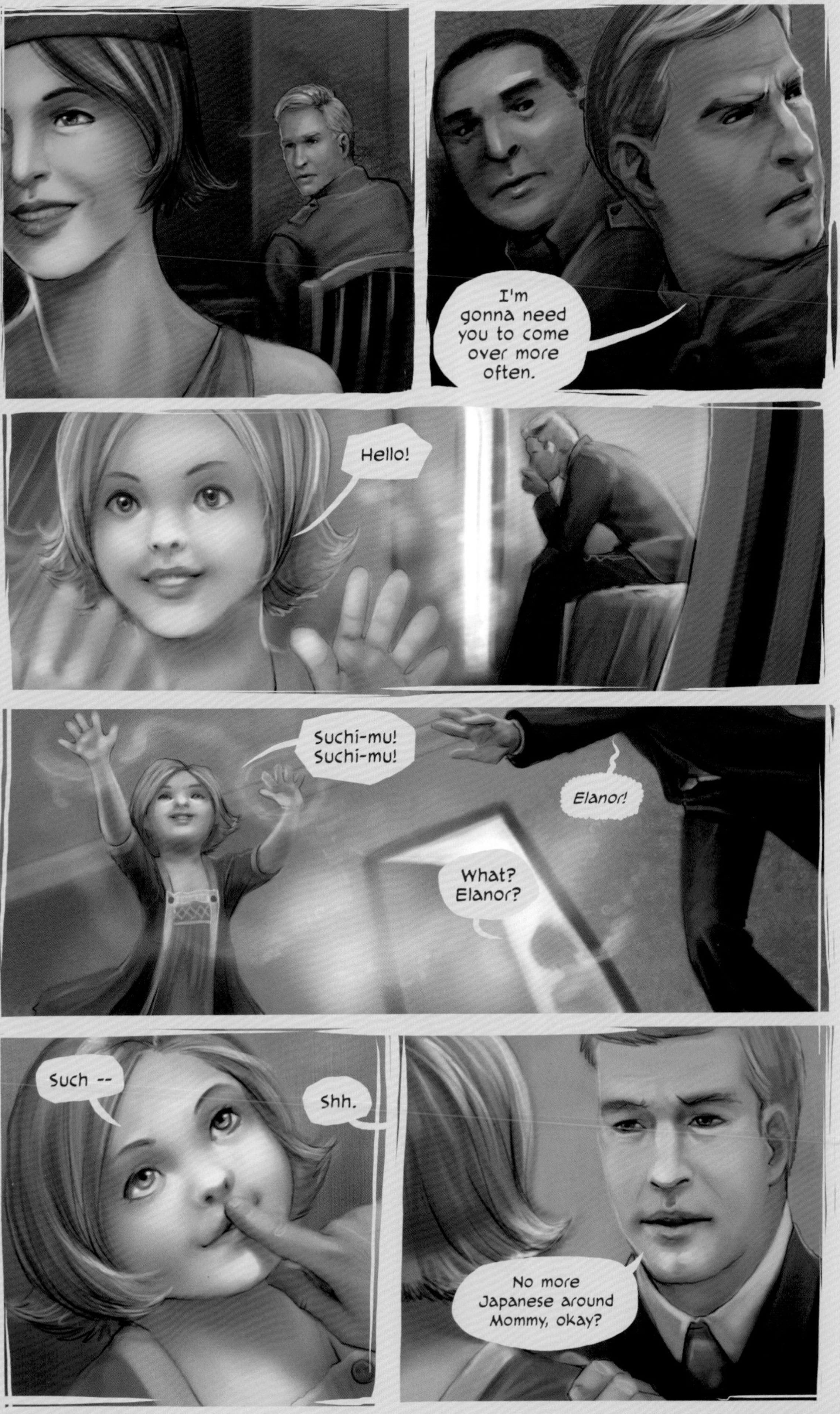
I'm gonna need you to come over more often.
Hello!
Suchi-mu! Suchi-mu!
Elanor!
What? Elanor?
Such --
Shh.
No more Japanese around Mommy, okay?

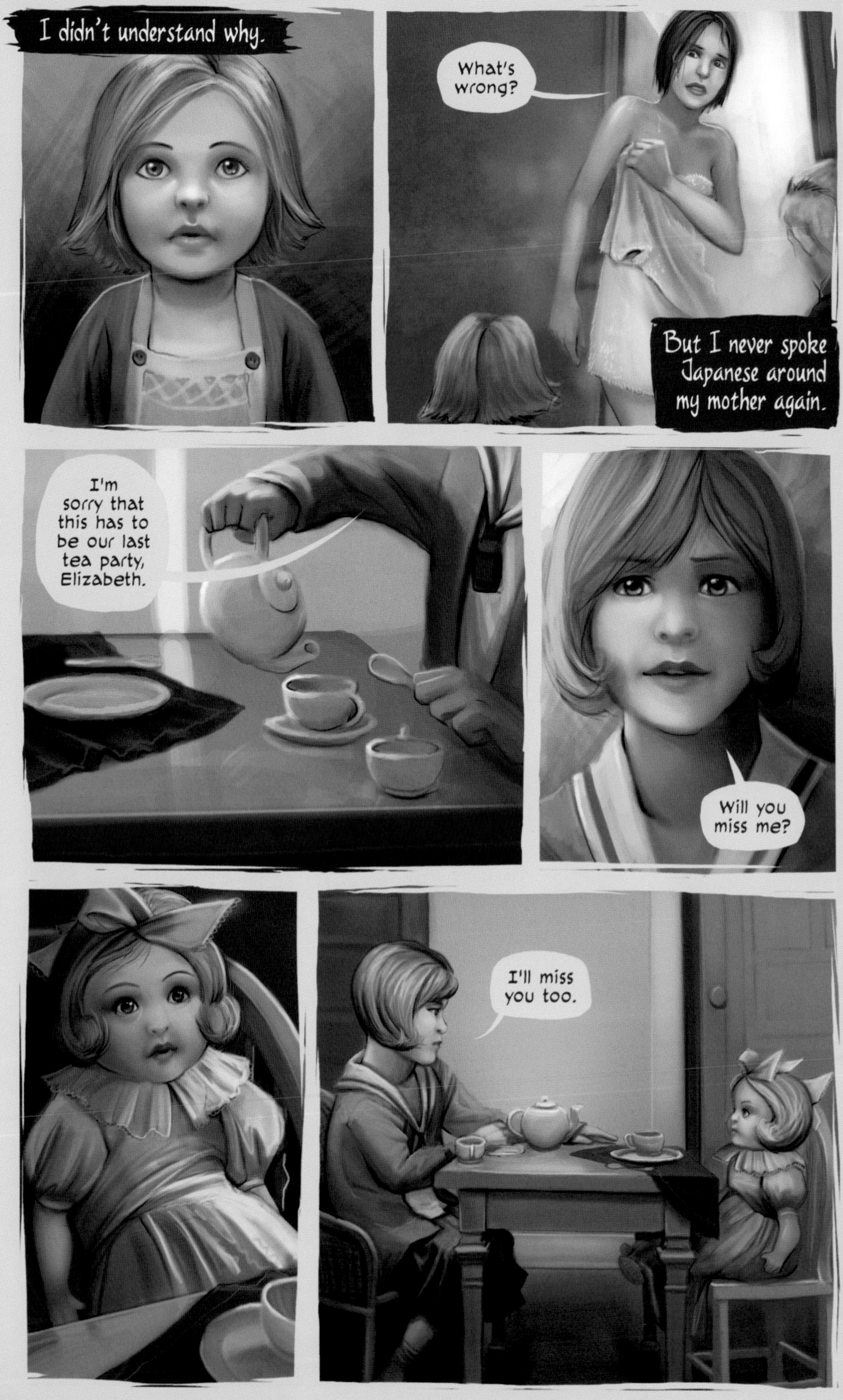
I didn't understand why.
What's wrong?
But I never spoke Japanese around my mother again.
I'm sorry that this has to be our last tea party, Elizabeth.
Will you miss me?
I'll miss you too.

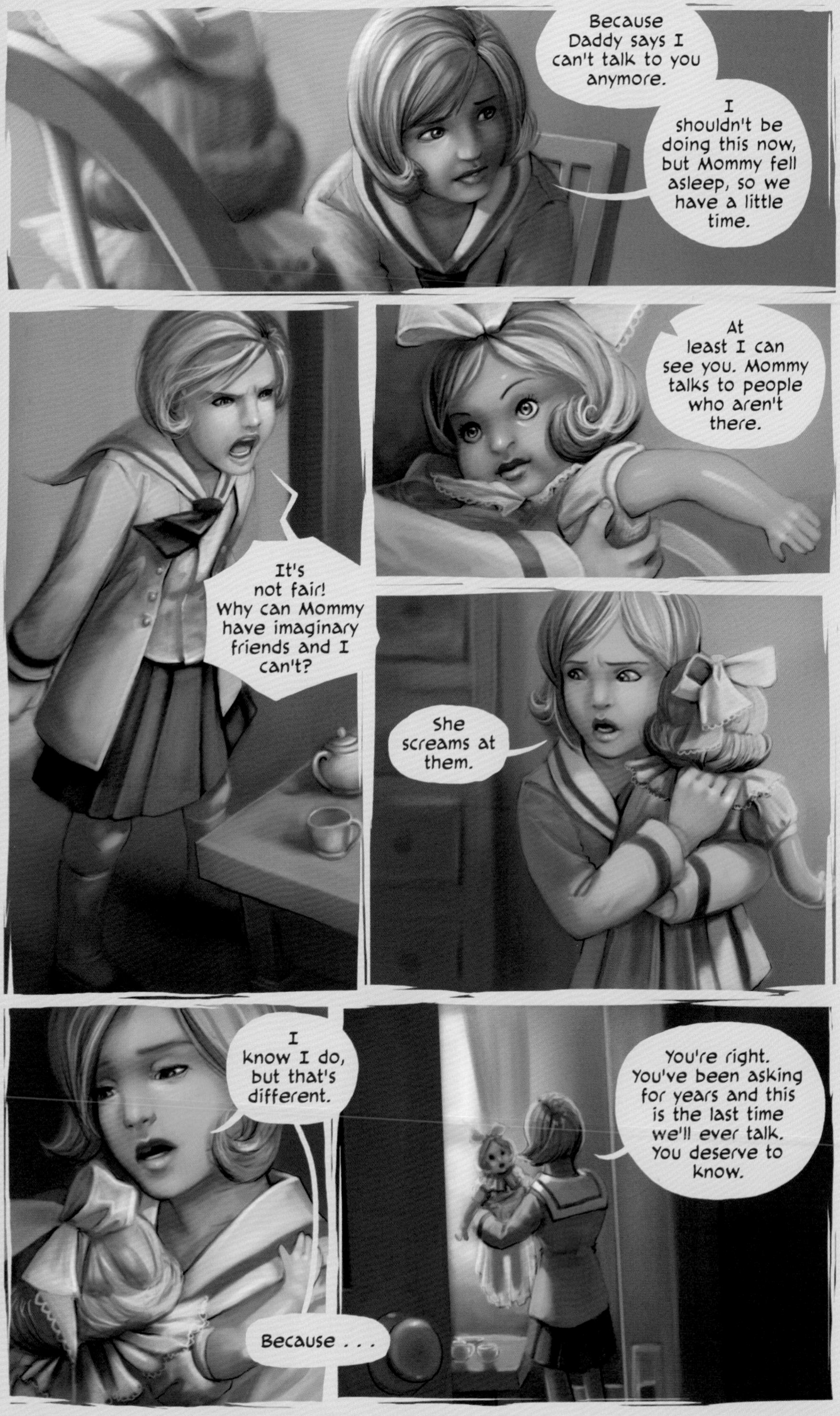
Because Daddy says I can't talk to you anymore.
I shouldn't be doing this now, but Mommy fell asleep, so we have a little time.
It's not fair! Why can Mommy have imaginary friends and I can't?
At least I can see you. Mommy talks to people who aren't there.
She screams at them.
I know I do, but that's different.
Because . . .
You're right. You've been asking for years and this is the last time we'll ever talk. You deserve to know.

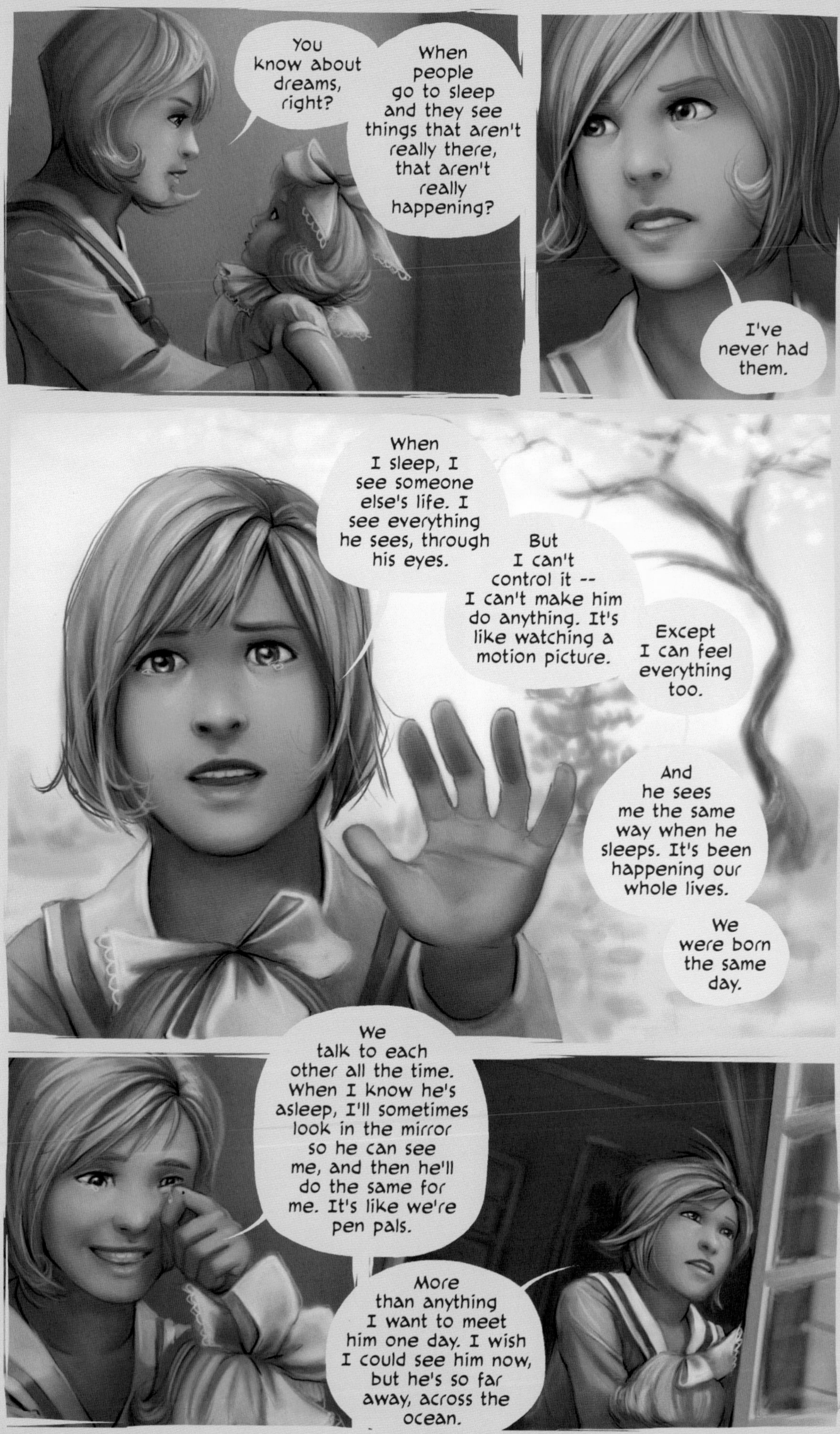
You know about dreams, right?
When people go to sleep and they see things that aren't really there, that aren't really happening?
I've never had them.
When I sleep, I see someone else's life. I see everything he sees, through his eyes.
But I can't control it -- I can't make him do anything. It's like watching a motion picture.
Except I can feel everything too.
And he sees me the same way when he sleeps. It's been happening our whole lives.
We were born the same day.
We talk to each other all the time. When I know he's asleep, I'll sometimes look in the mirror so he can see me, and then he'll do the same for me. It's like we're pen pals.
More than anything I want to meet him one day. I wish I could see him now, but he's so far away, across the ocean.

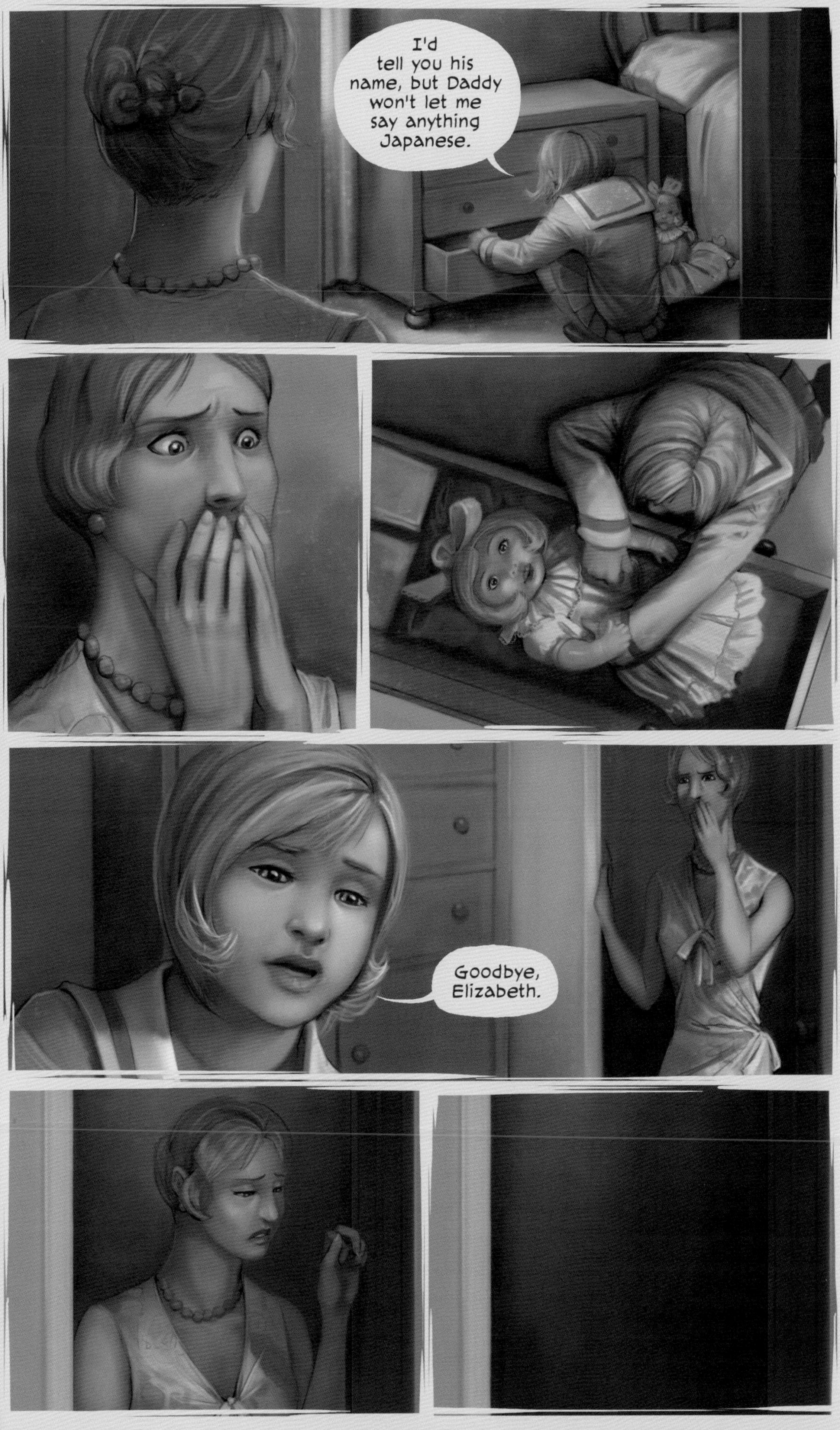
I'd tell you his name, but Daddy won't let me say anything Japanese.
Goodbye, Elizabeth.

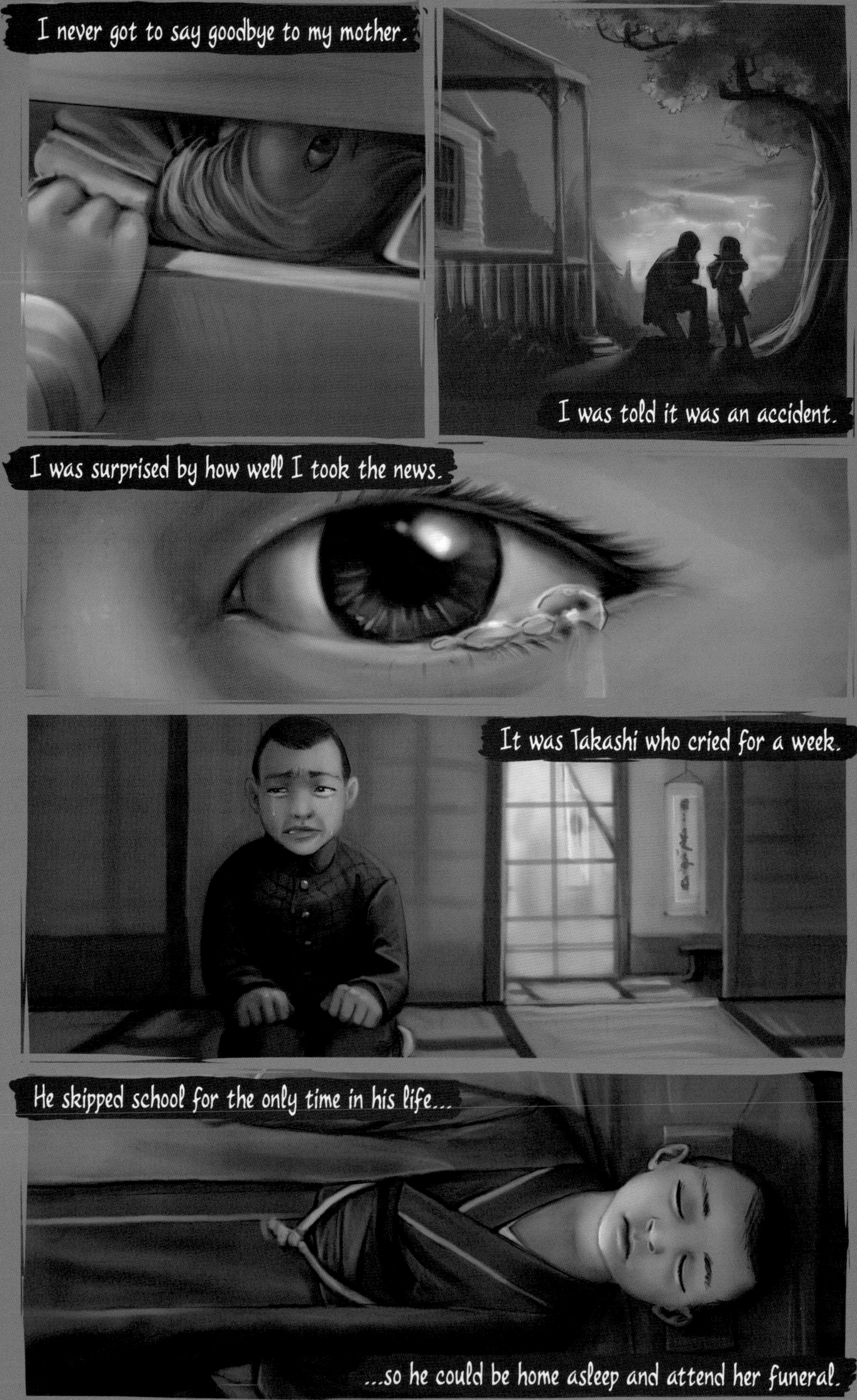
I never got to say goodbye to my mother.
I was told it was an accident.
I was surprised by how well I took the news.
It was Takashi who cried for a week.
He skipped school for the only time in his life...
...so he could be home asleep and attend her funeral.

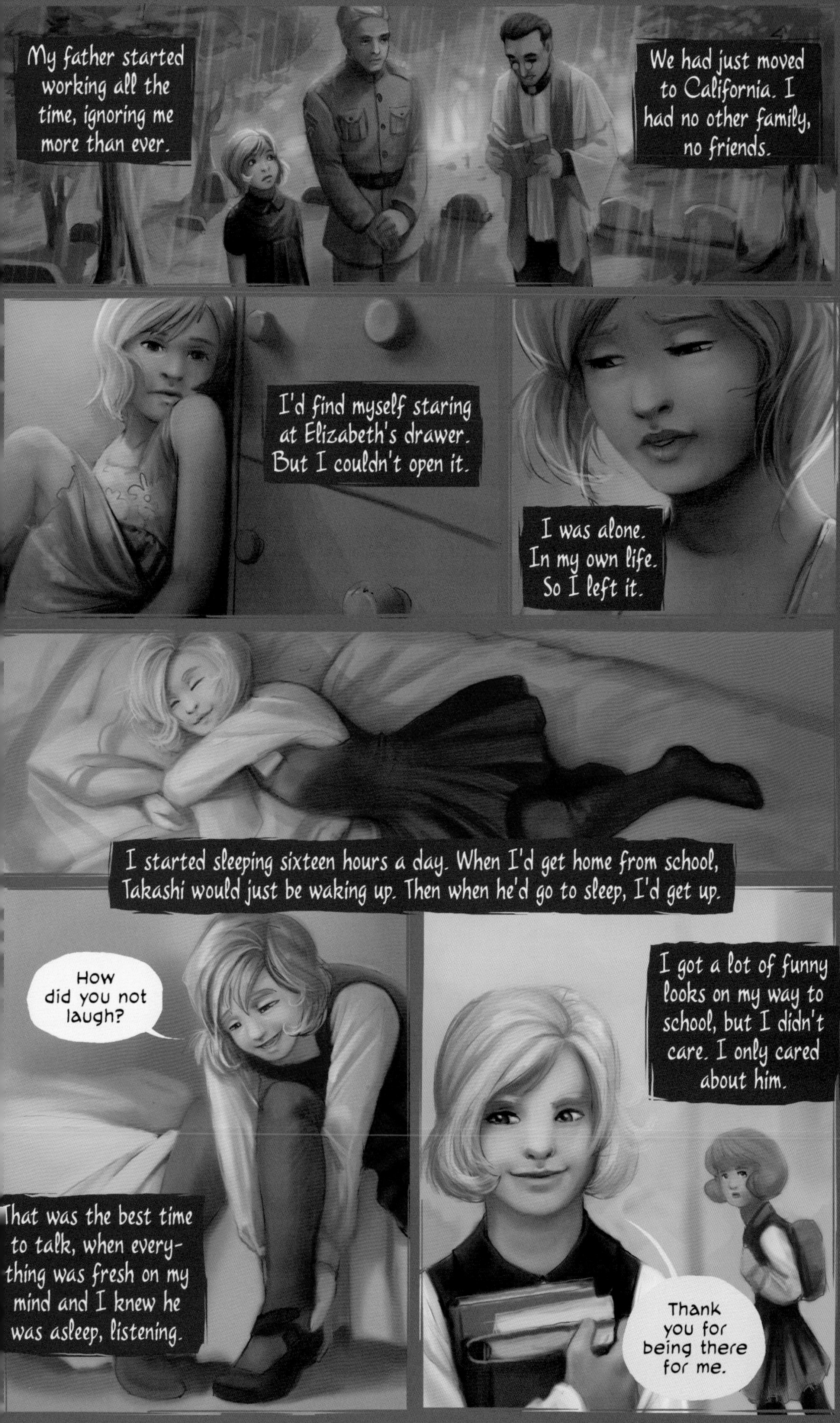
My father started working all the time, ignoring me more than ever.
We had just moved to California. I had no other family, no friends.
I'd find myself staring at Elizabeth's drawer. But I couldn't open it.
I was alone. In my own life. So I left it.
I started sleeping sixteen hours a day. When I'd get home from school, Takashi would just be waking up. Then when he'd go to sleep, I'd get up.
How did you not laugh?
That was the best time to talk, when everything was fresh on my mind and I knew he was asleep, listening.
I got a lot of funny looks on my way to school, but I didn't care. I only cared about him.
Thank you for being there for me.

I stopped paying attention in class.

I don't know why I even went.

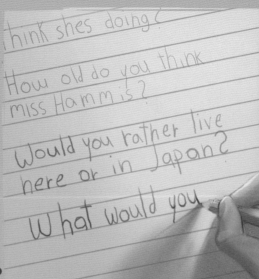

think shes doing?

How old do you think miss Hamm is?

Would you rather live here or in Japan?

What would you

He tried to answer all my questions, but it's hard to remember them hours later.

Miss Hamm is 43!

Over time I got to know him so well that I didn't need to ask him anything.

I was spending most of my life as him. We were closer than any two people have ever been, while living over five thousand miles apart.

I wish you were here

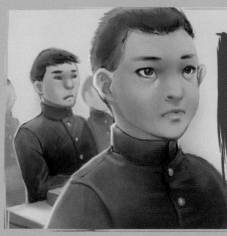

We matured quickly, living full twenty-four hour days in two countries with two educations. There was no time off, no breaks.

I hated when we were both asleep. I'd just see darkness and hear the sounds of his room. It made me feel lonely, vulnerable.

I forced myself awake whenever that happened.

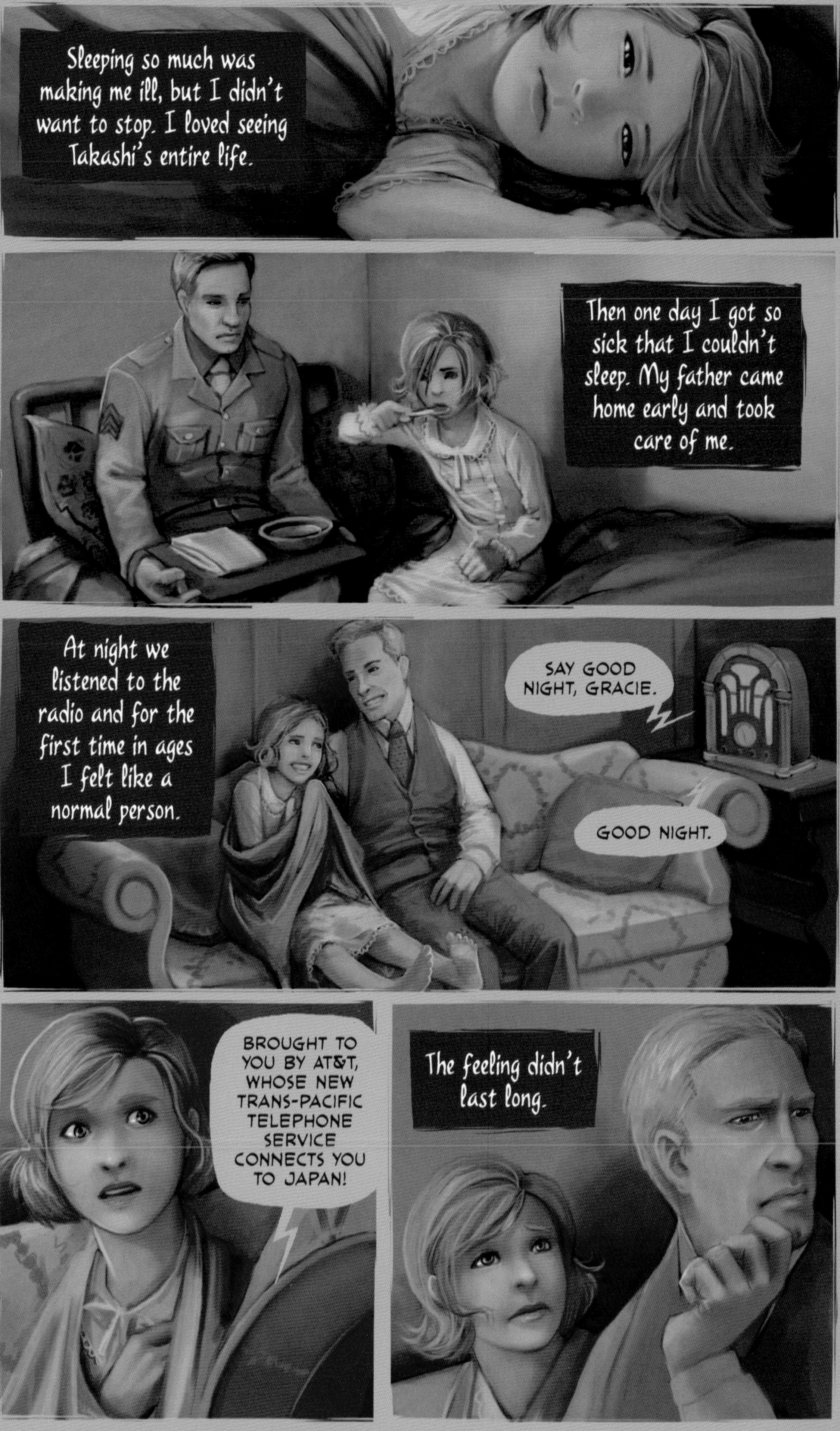
Sleeping so much was making me ill, but I didn't want to stop. I loved seeing Takashi's entire life.
Then one day I got so sick that I couldn't sleep. My father came home early and took care of me.
At night we listened to the radio and for the first time in ages I felt like a normal person.
SAY GOOD NIGHT, GRACIE.
GOOD NIGHT.
BROUGHT TO YOU BY AT&T, WHOSE NEW TRANS-PACIFIC TELEPHONE SERVICE CONNECTS YOU TO JAPAN!
The feeling didn't last long.

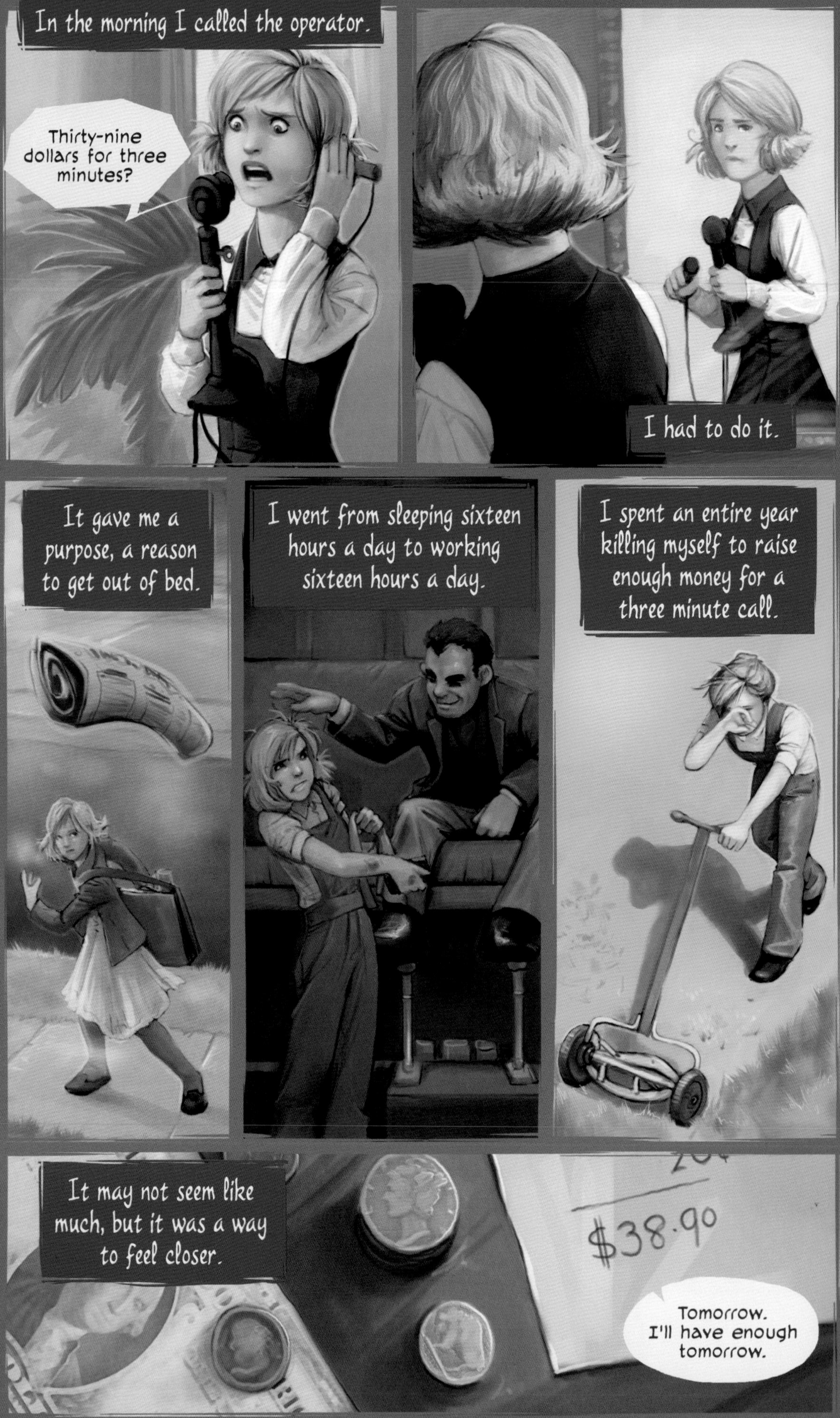
In the morning I called the operator.
Thirty-nine dollars for three minutes?
I had to do it.
It gave me a purpose, a reason to get out of bed.
I went from sleeping sixteen hours a day to working sixteen hours a day.
I spent an entire year killing myself to raise enough money for a three minute call.
It may not seem like much, but it was a way to feel closer.
$38.90
Tomorrow. I'll have enough tomorrow.

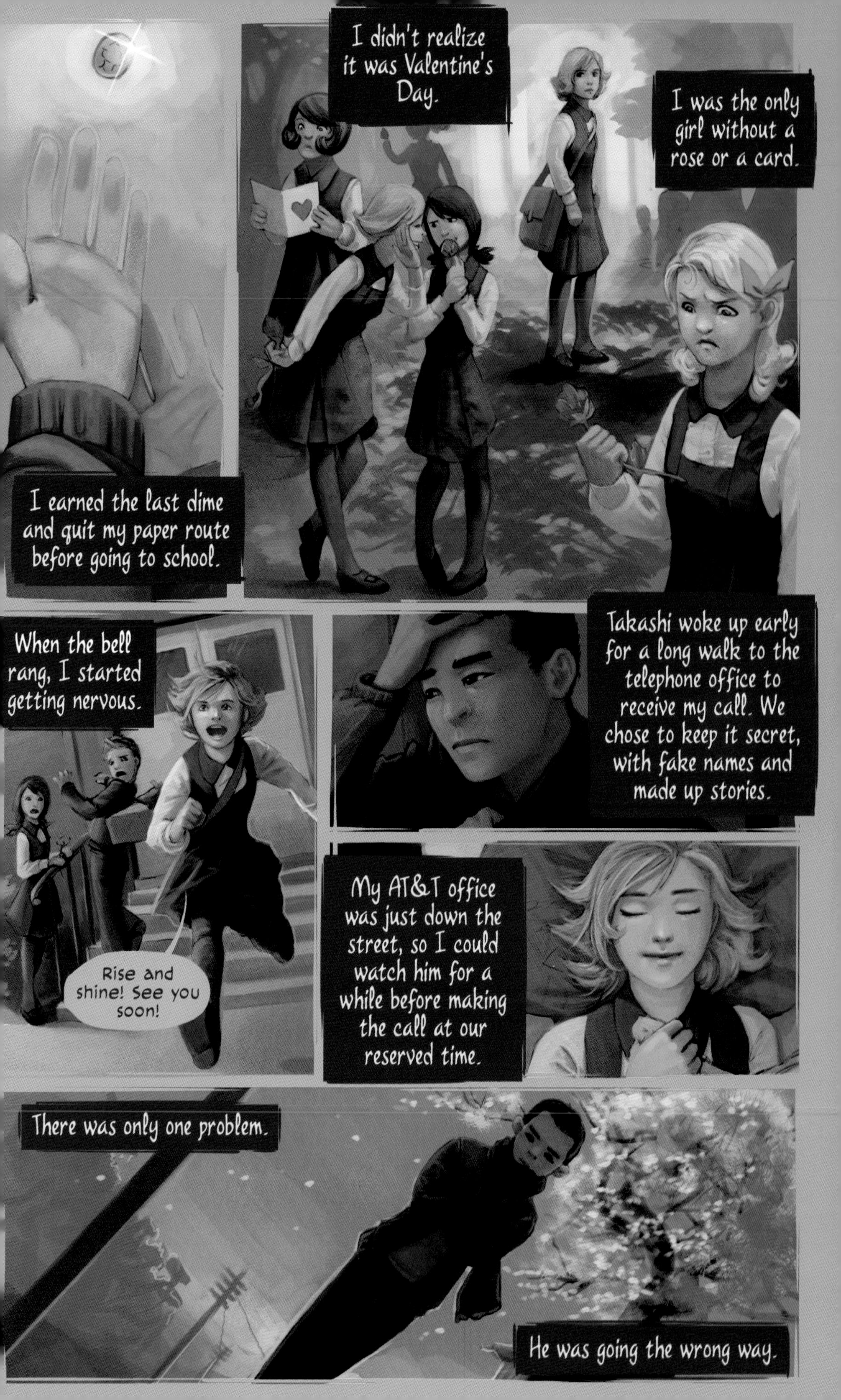
I earned the last dime and quit my paper route before going to school.
I didn't realize it was Valentine's Day.
I was the only girl without a rose or a card.
When the bell rang, I started getting nervous.
Rise and shine! See you soon!
Takashi woke up early for a long walk to the telephone office to receive my call. We chose to keep it secret, with fake names and made up stories.
My AT&T office was just down the street, so I could watch him for a while before making the call at our reserved time.
There was only one problem.
He was going the wrong way.

I'd never seen this place before. He must have went here when I was awake.

Time was running out. I didn't understand.

I know why you want to call me.

You're scared that I'm not real... that I'm just in your head... that you're like your mother.

But there's a better way to prove it. It's in your mailbox right now.

I held it ten seconds later.

A water lily, suiren in Japanese. It means "far from the one he loves."

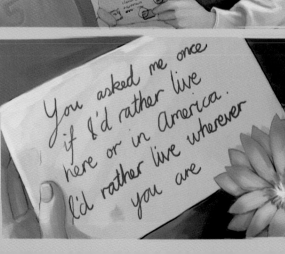

You asked me once if I'd rather live here or in America. I'd rather live wherever you are

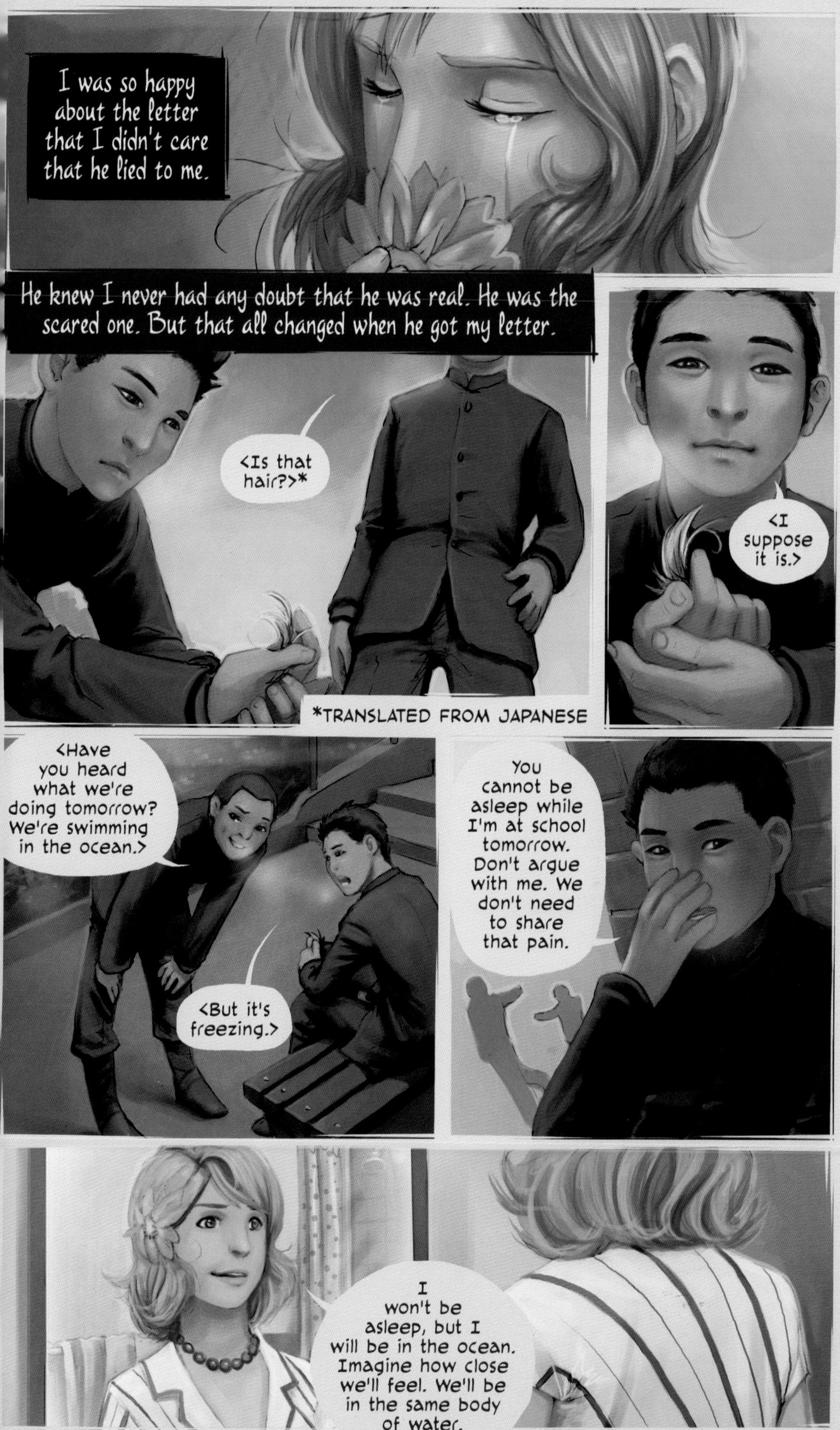
I was so happy about the letter that I didn't care that he lied to me.
He knew I never had any doubt that he was real. He was the scared one. But that all changed when he got my letter.
<Is that hair?>*
<I suppose it is.>
*TRANSLATED FROM JAPANESE
<Have you heard what we're doing tomorrow? We're swimming in the ocean.>
<But it's freezing.>
You cannot be asleep while I'm at school tomorrow. Don't argue with me. We don't need to share that pain.
I won't be asleep, but I will be in the ocean. Imagine how close we'll feel. We'll be in the same body of water.

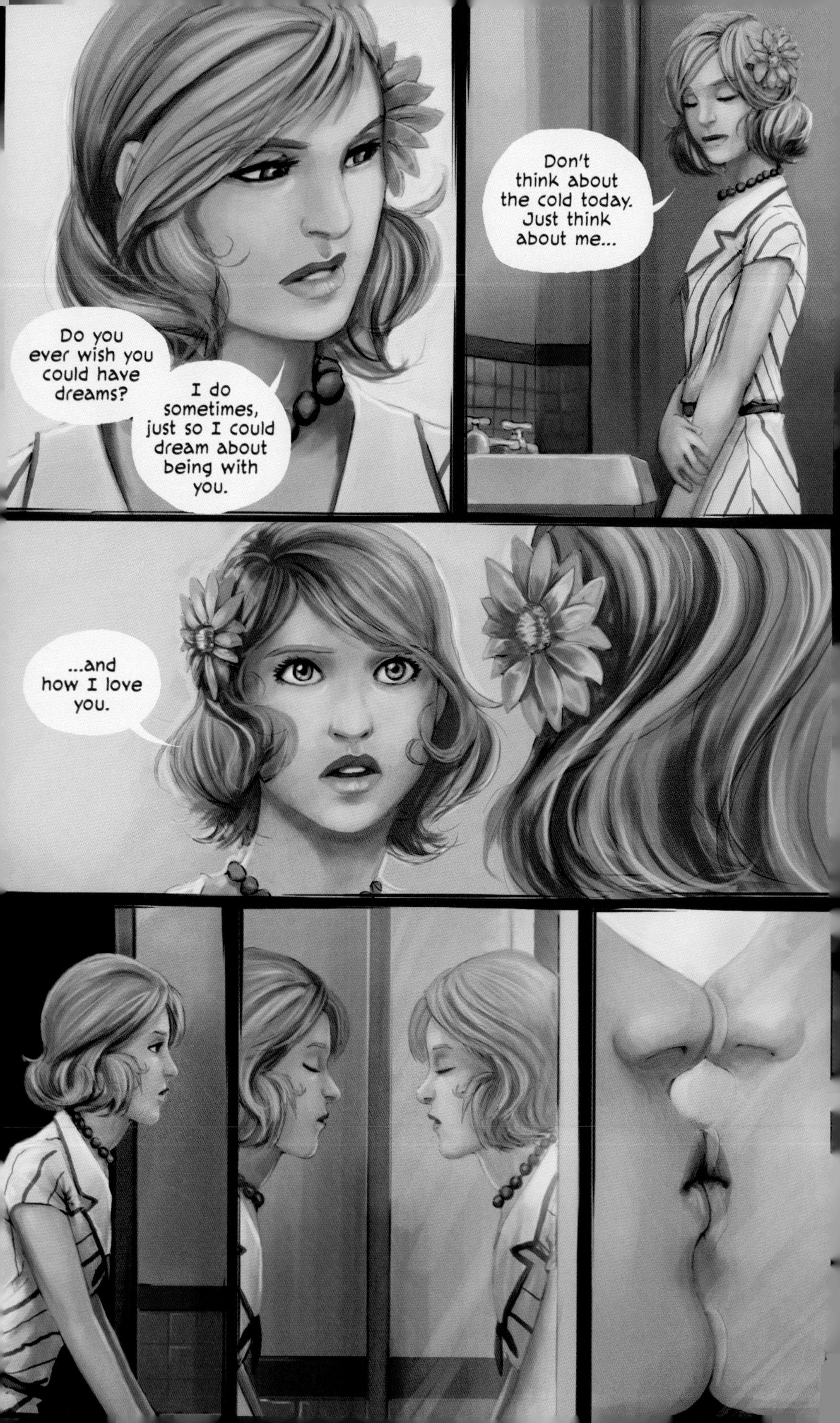
Do you ever wish you could have dreams?
I do sometimes, just so I could dream about being with you.
Don't think about the cold today. Just think about me...
...and how I love you.

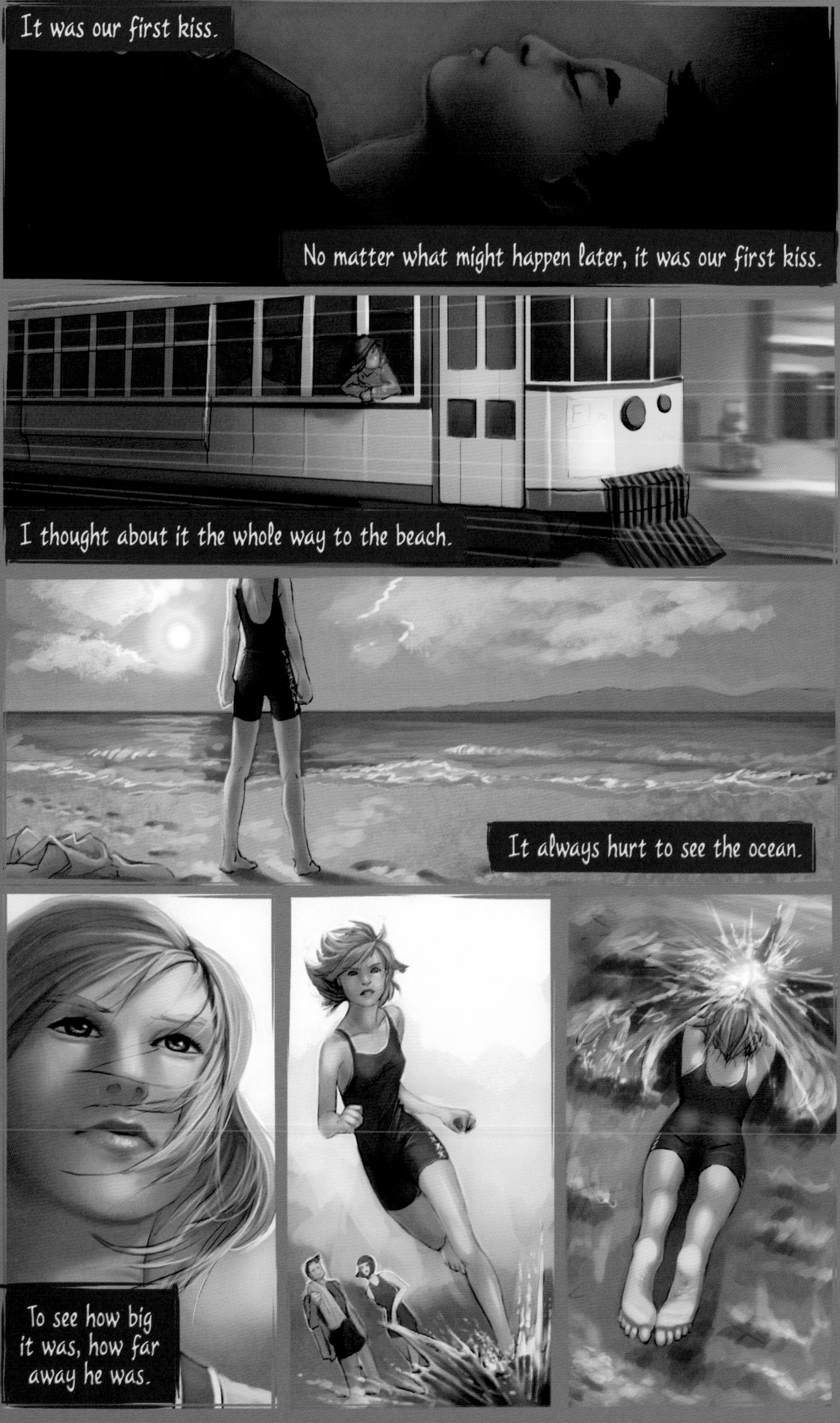
It was our first kiss.
No matter what might happen later, it was our first kiss.
I thought about it the whole way to the beach.
It always hurt to see the ocean.
To see how big it was, how far away he was.

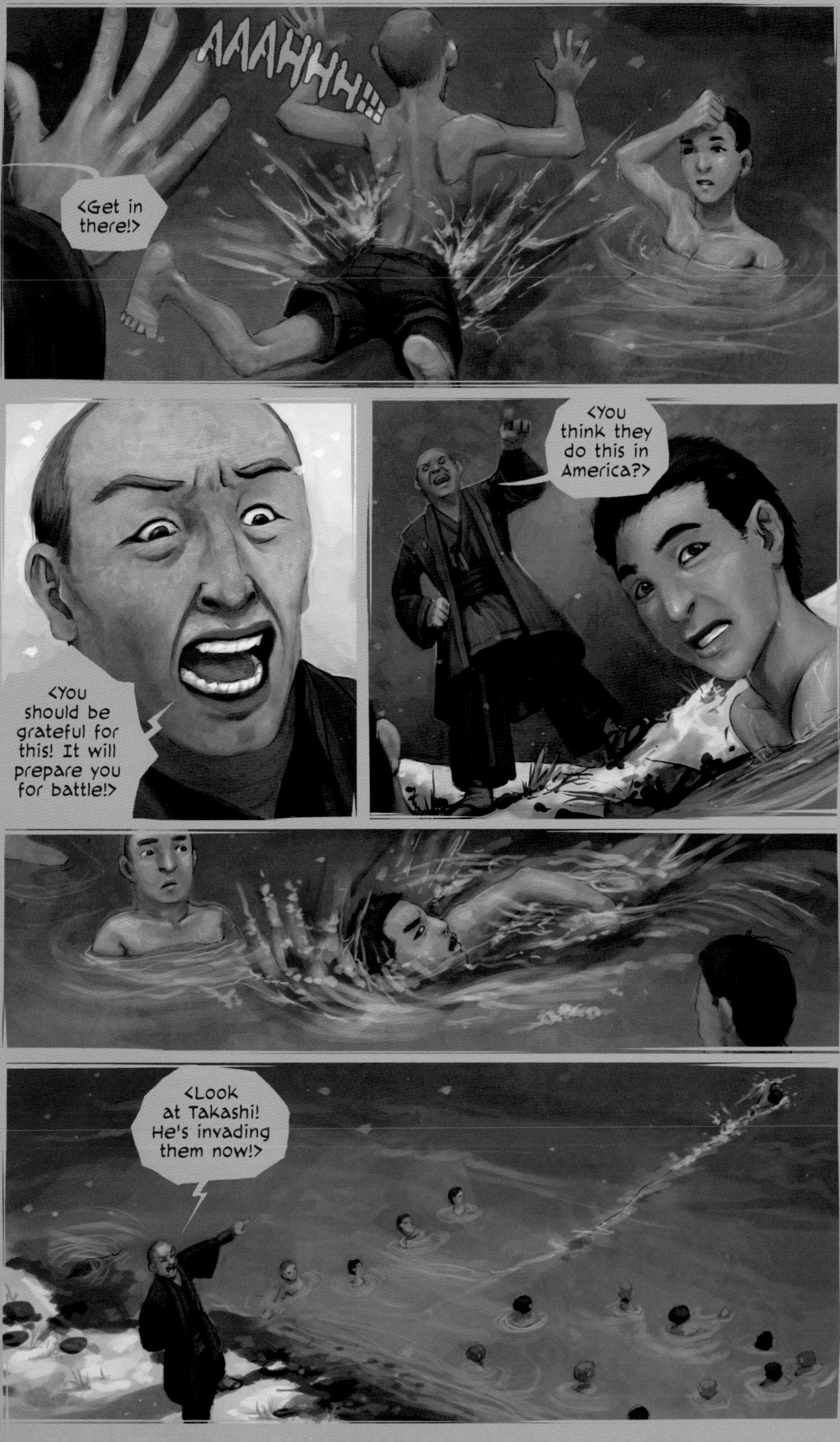
AAAHHH!!!
<Get in there!>
<You should be grateful for this! It will prepare you for battle!>
<You think they do this in America?>
<Look at Takashi! He's invading them now!>

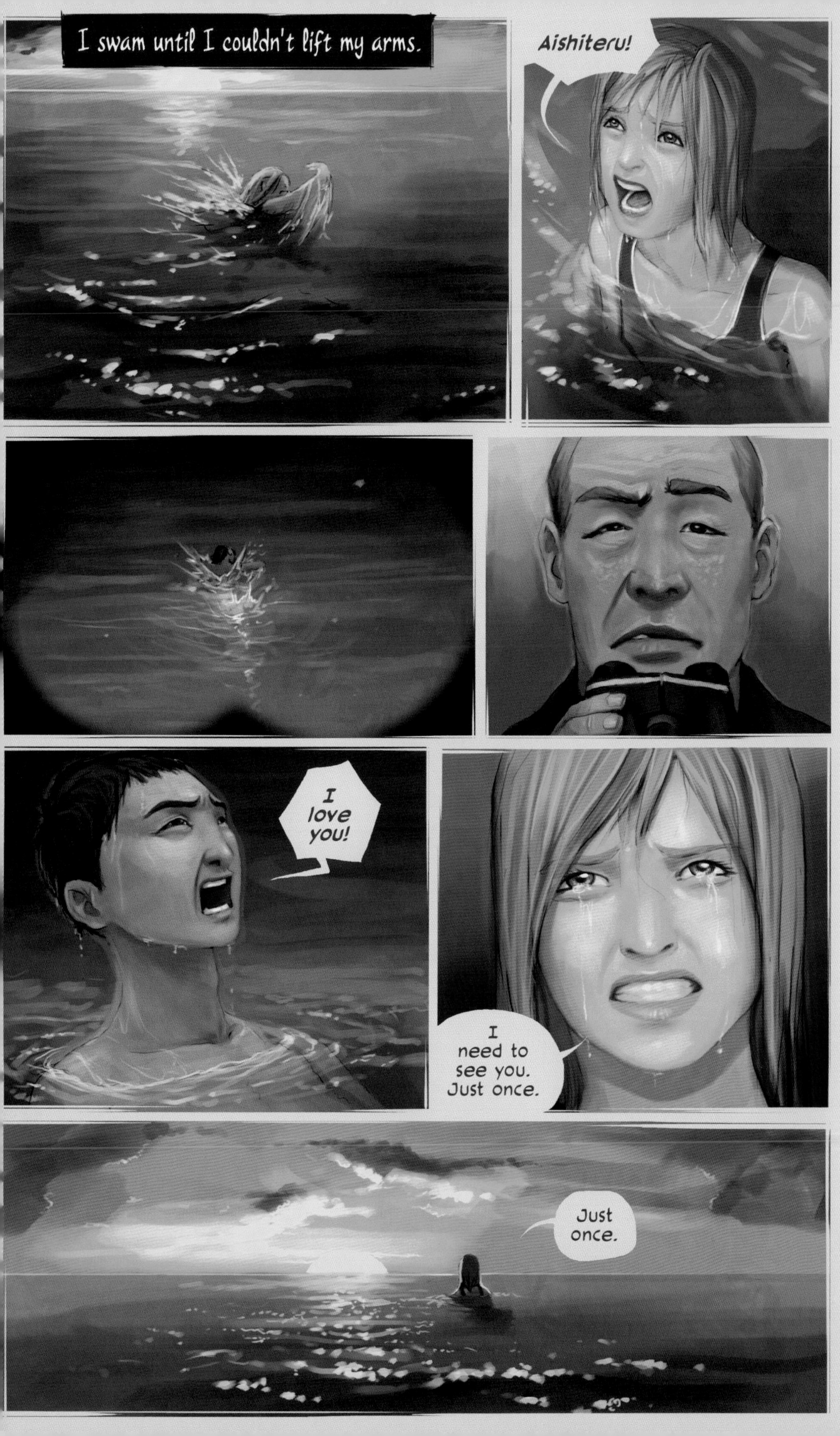
I swam until I couldn't lift my arms.
Aishiteru!
I love you!
I need to see you. Just once.
Just once.

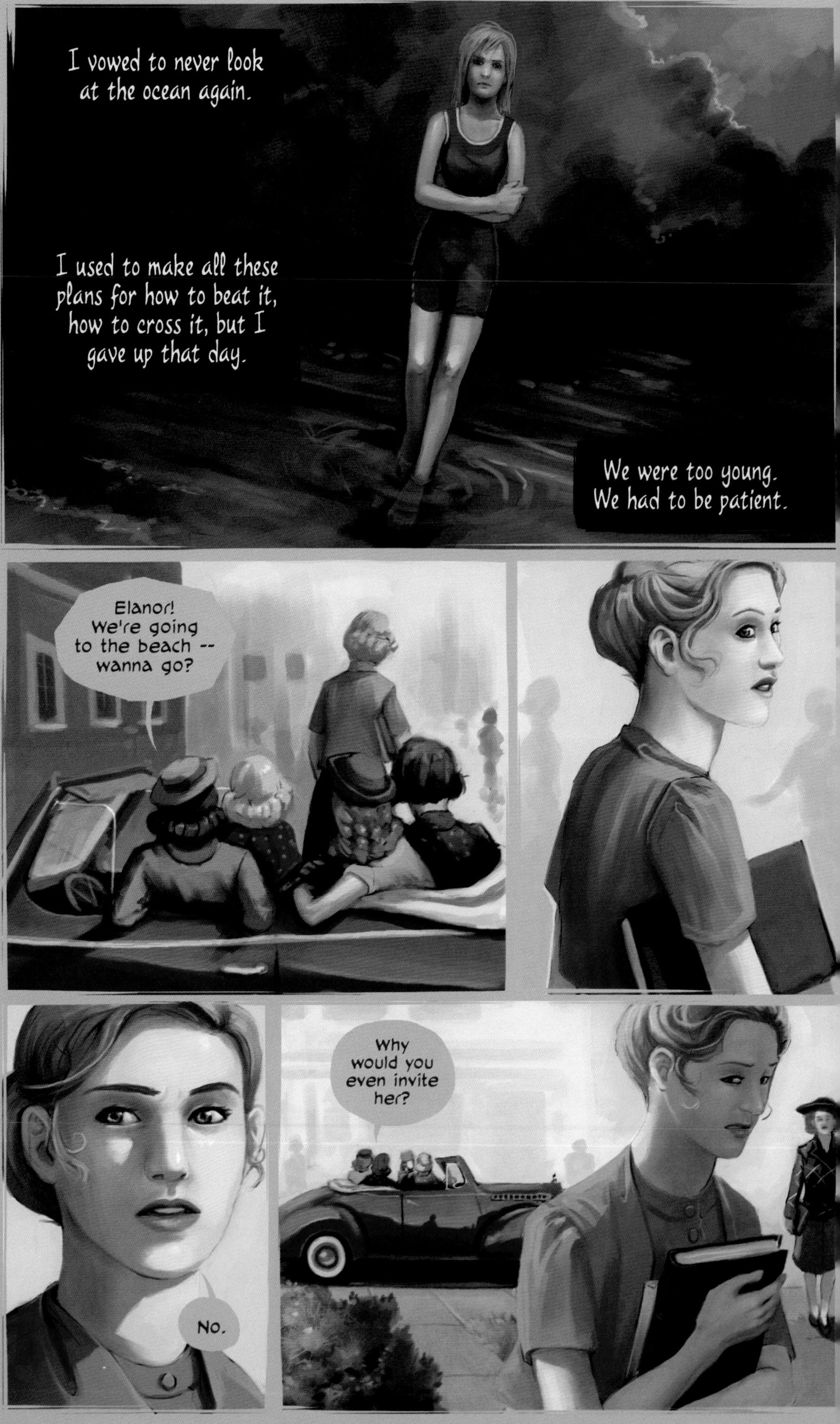
I vowed to never look at the ocean again.
I used to make all these plans for how to beat it, how to cross it, but I gave up that day.
We were too young. We had to be patient.
Elanor! We're going to the beach -- wanna go?
No.
Why would you even invite her?

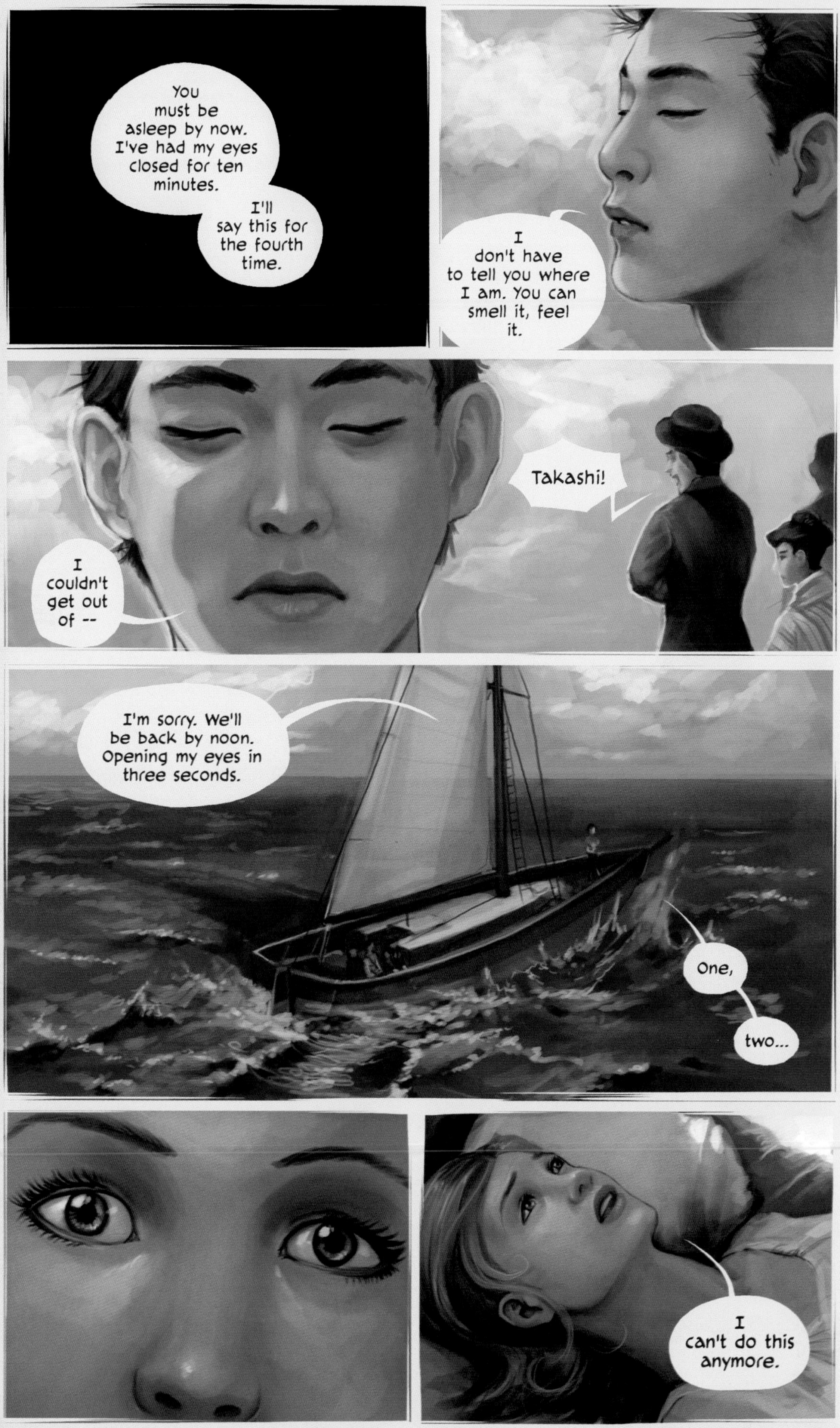
You must be asleep by now. I've had my eyes closed for ten minutes.
I'll say this for the fourth time.
I don't have to tell you where I am. You can smell it, feel it.
I couldn't get out of --
Takashi!
I'm sorry. We'll be back by noon. Opening my eyes in three seconds.
One,
two...
I can't do this anymore.

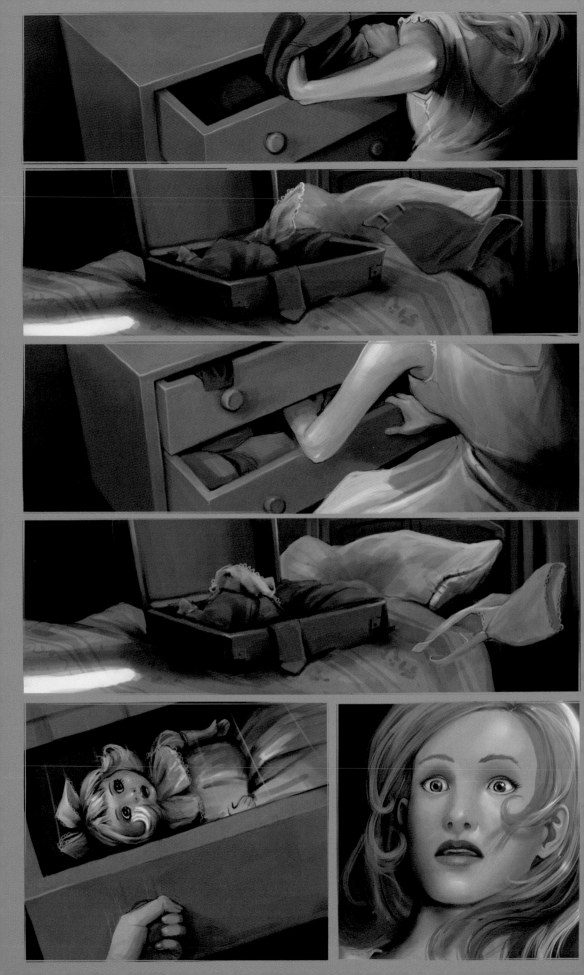

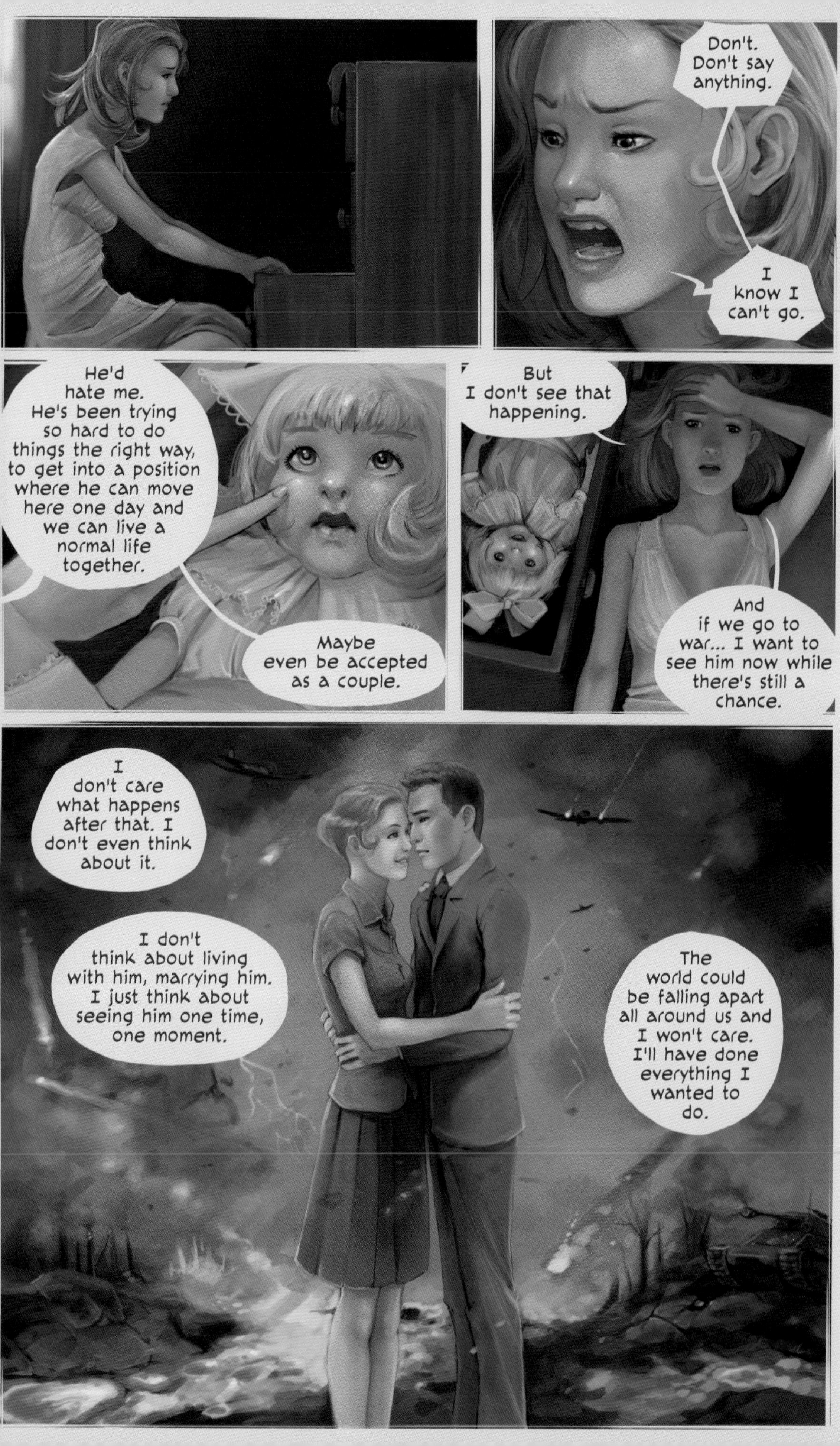
Don't. Don't say anything.
I know I can't go.
He'd hate me. He's been trying so hard to do things the right way, to get into a position where he can move here one day and we can live a normal life together.
Maybe even be accepted as a couple.
But I don't see that happening.
And if we go to war... I want to see him now while there's still a chance.
I don't care what happens after that. I don't even think about it.
I don't think about living with him, marrying him. I just think about seeing him one time, one moment.
The world could be falling apart all around us and I won't care. I'll have done everything I wanted to do.

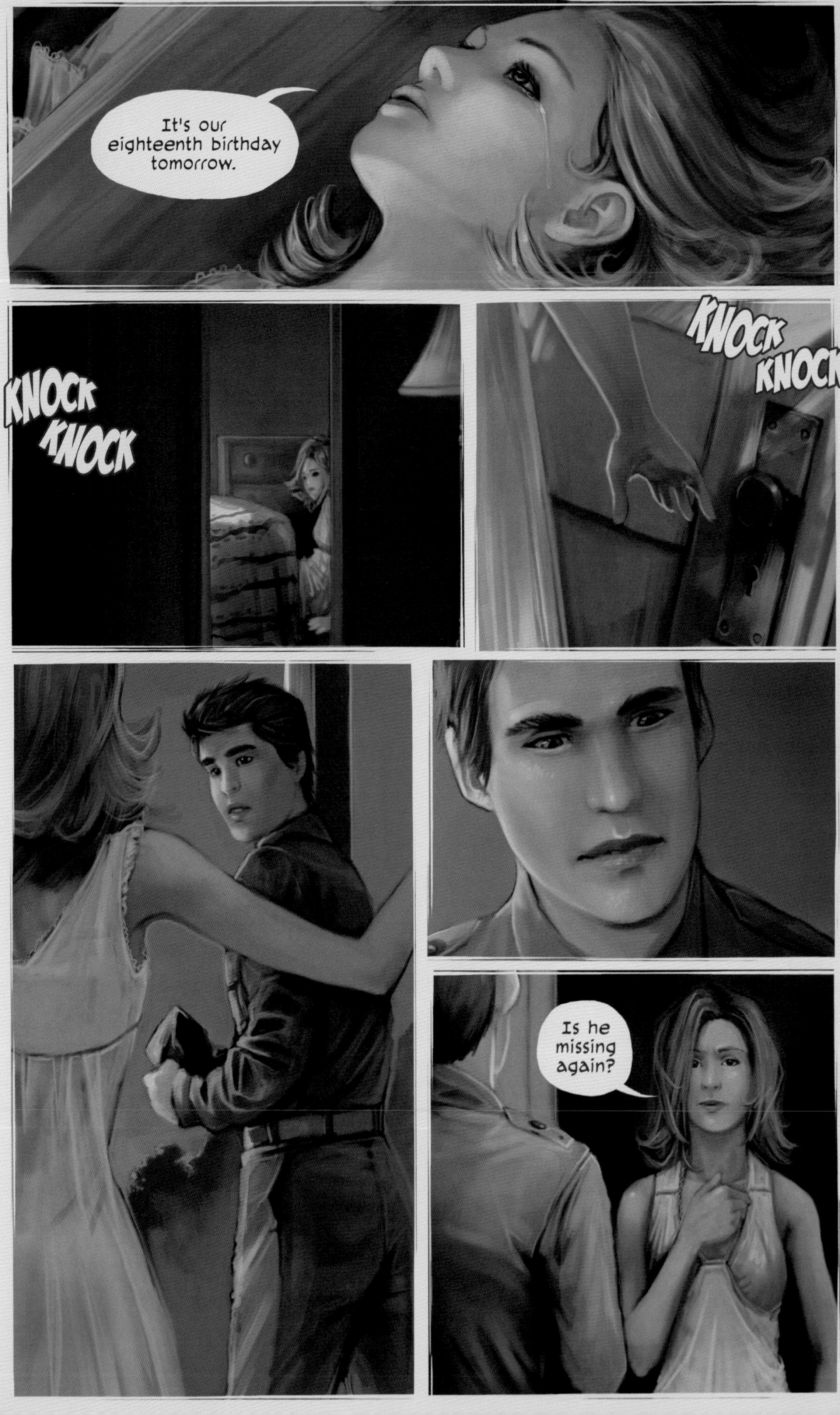
It's our eighteenth birthday tomorrow.
KNOCK KNOCK
KNOCK KNOCK
Is he missing again?

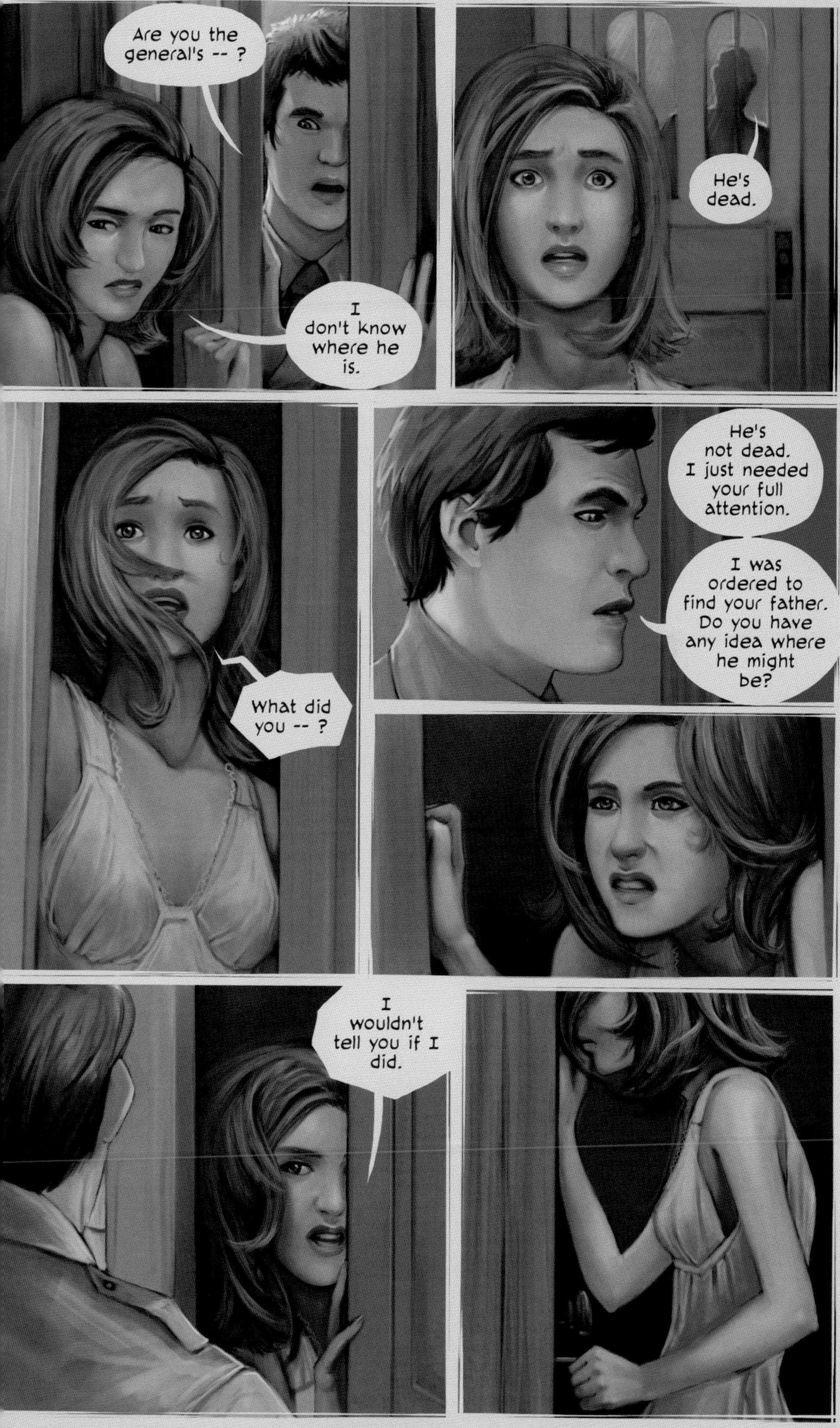
Are you the general's -- ?
I don't know where he is.
He's dead.
What did you -- ?
He's not dead. I just needed your full attention.
I was ordered to find your father. Do you have any idea where he might be?
I wouldn't tell you if I did.

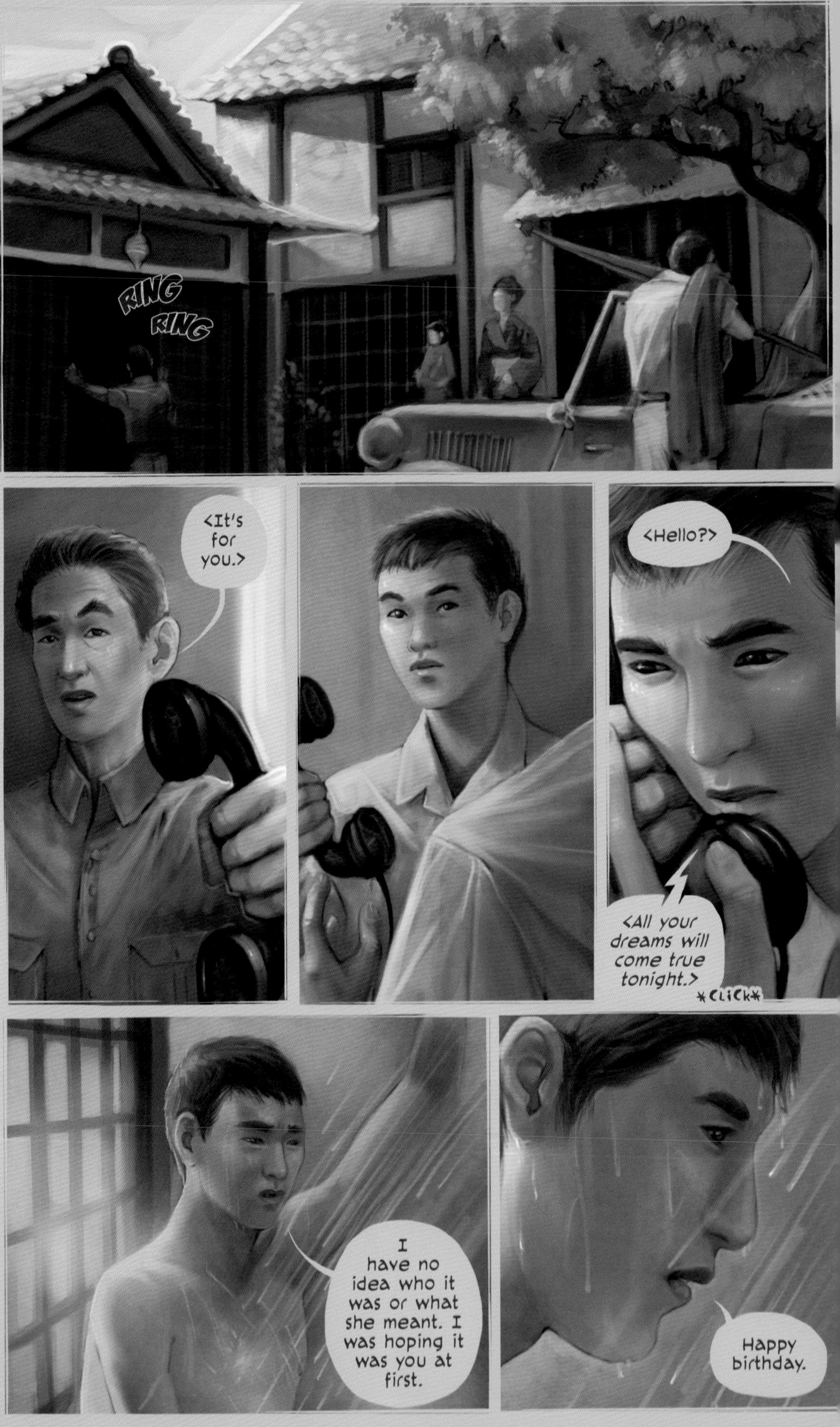
RING
RING
<It's for you.>
<Hello?>
<All your dreams will come true tonight.>
CLICK
I have no idea who it was or what she meant. I was hoping it was you at first.
Happy birthday.

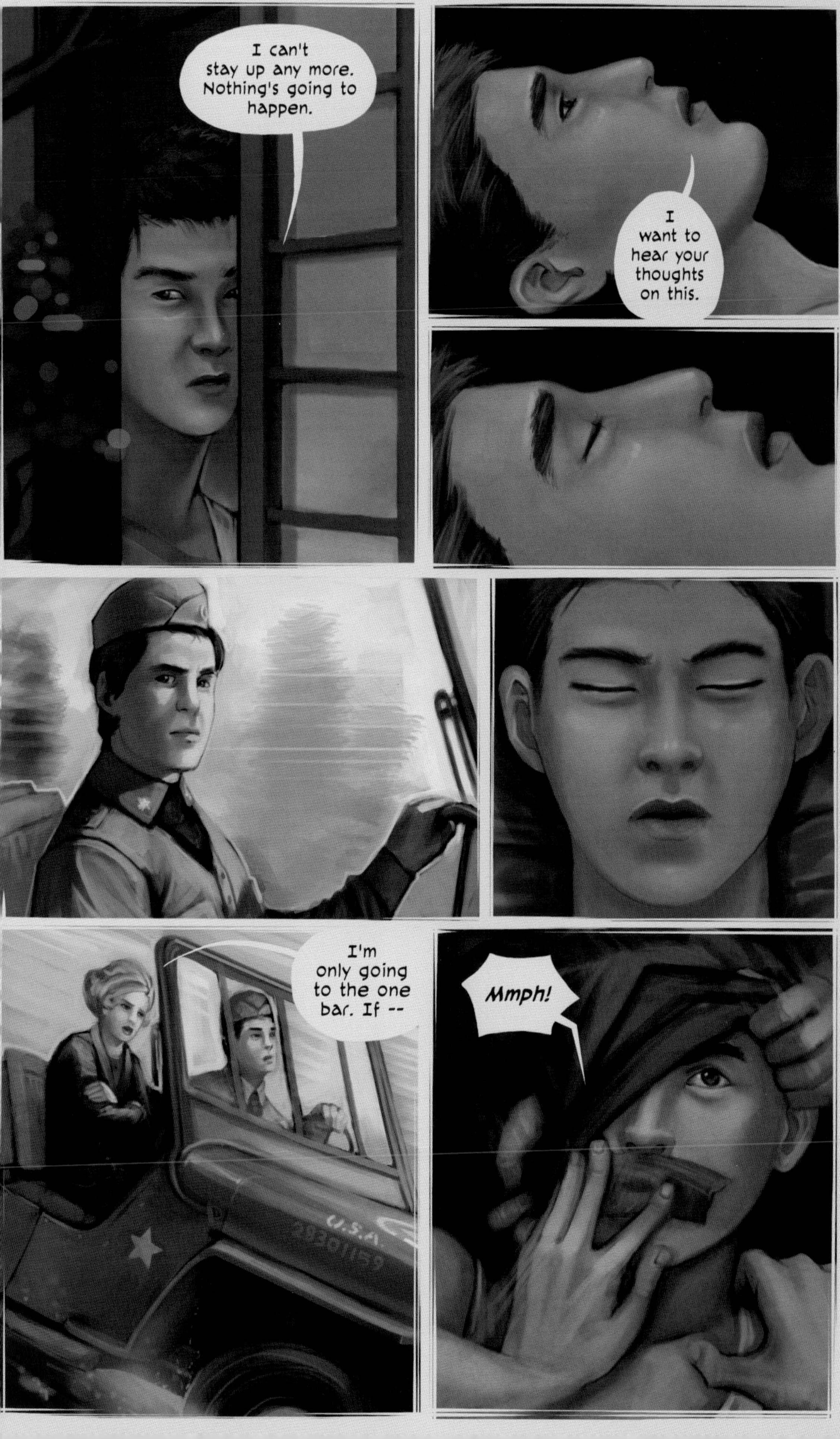
I can't stay up any more. Nothing's going to happen.
I want to hear your thoughts on this.
I'm only going to the one bar. If --
Mmph!
U.S.A.

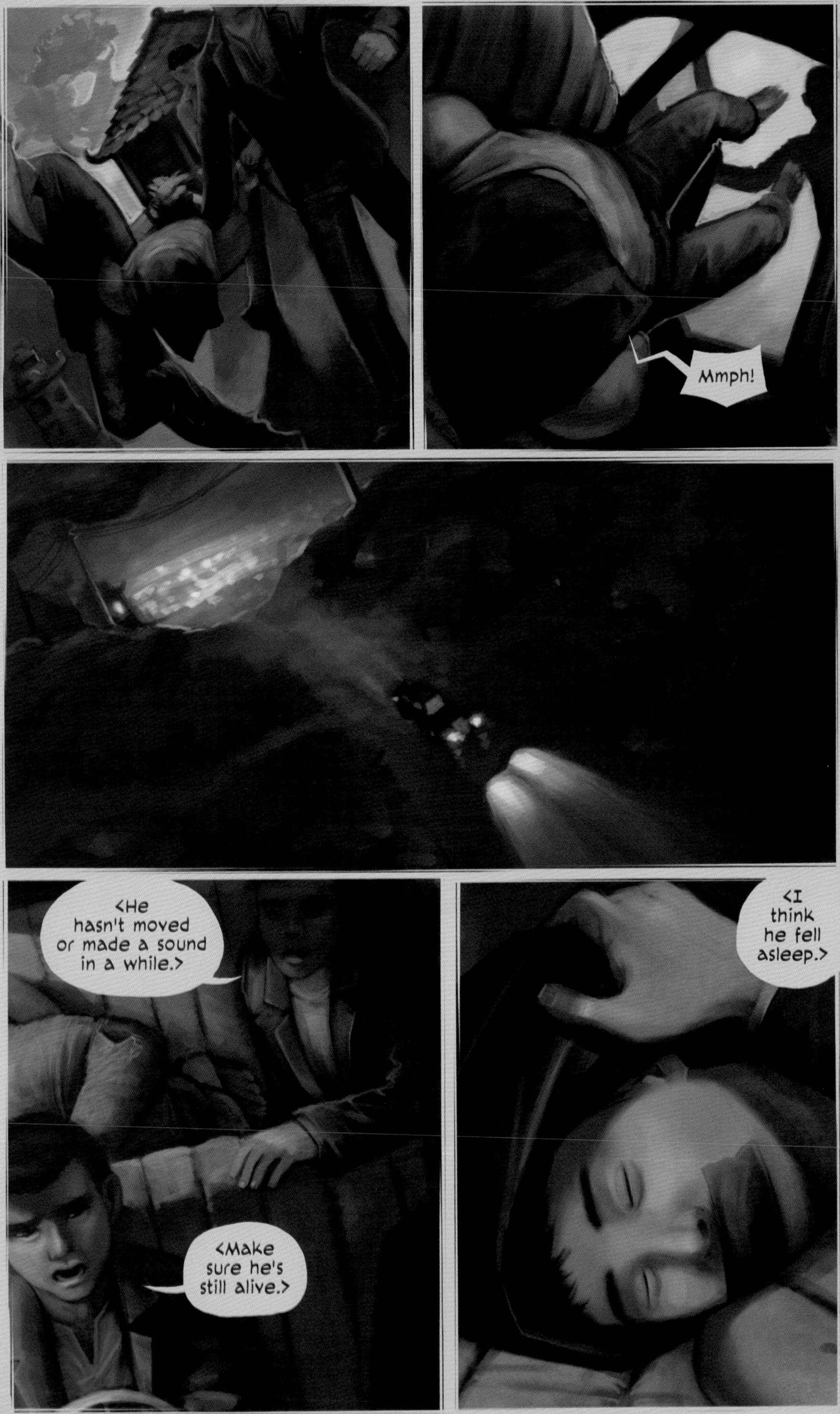
Mmph!
<He hasn't moved or made a sound in a while.>
<Make sure he's still alive.>
<I think he fell asleep.>

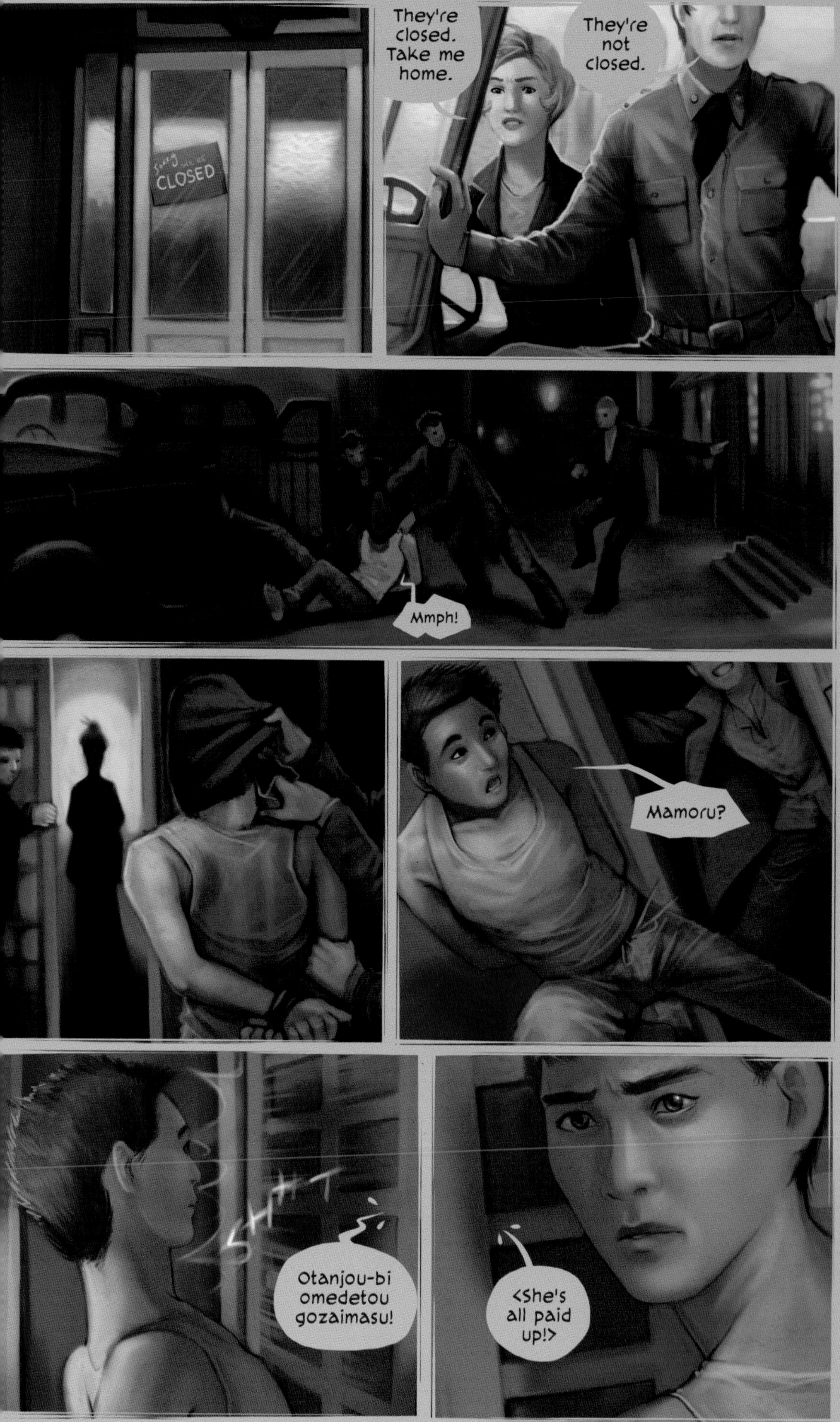
CLOSED
They're closed. Take me home.
They're not closed.
Mmph!
Mamoru?
SHHT
Otanjou-bi omedetou gozaimasu!
<She's all paid up!>

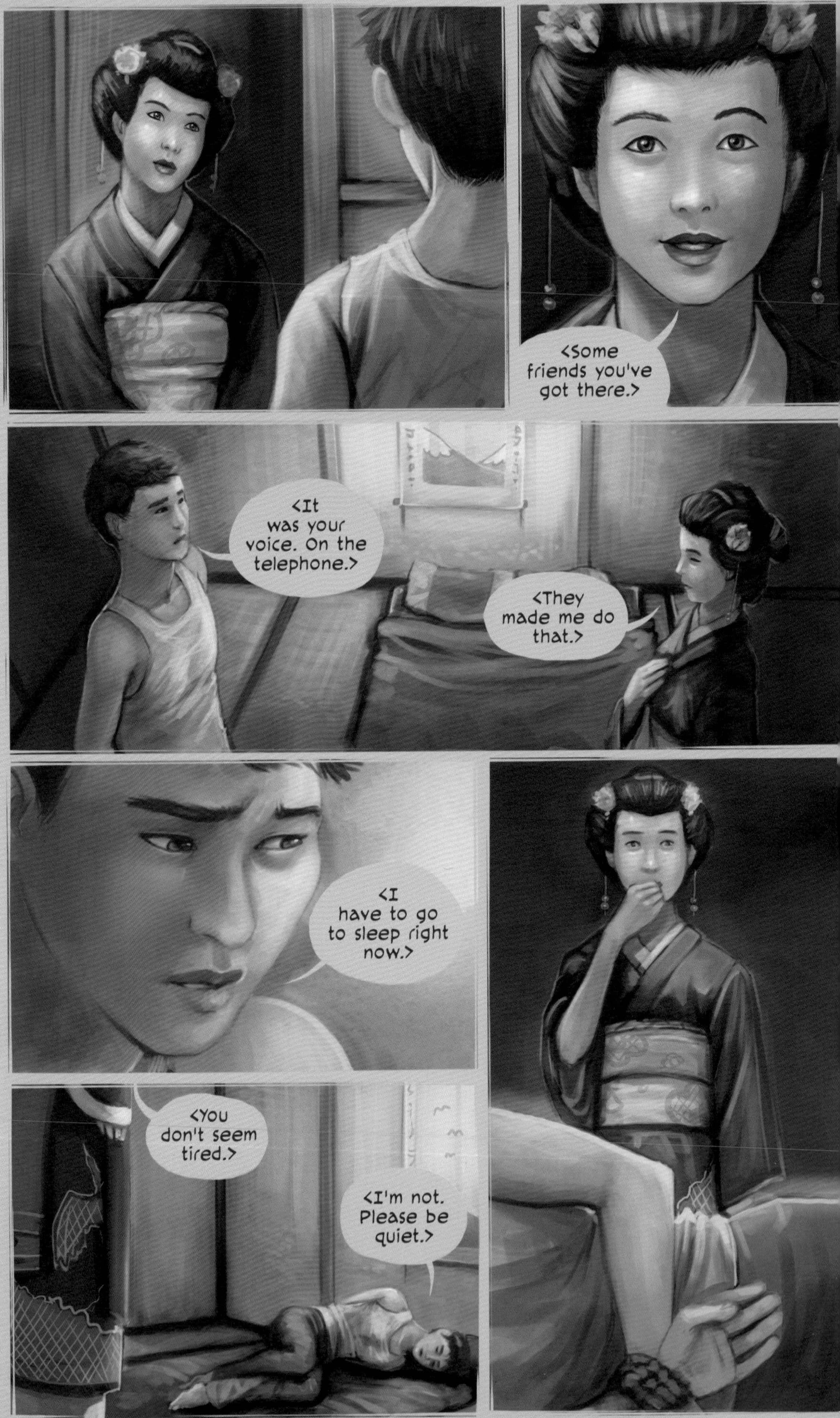

<Some friends you've got there.>
<It was your voice. On the telephone.>
<They made me do that.>
<I have to go to sleep right now.>
<You don't seem tired.>
<I'm not. Please be quiet.>

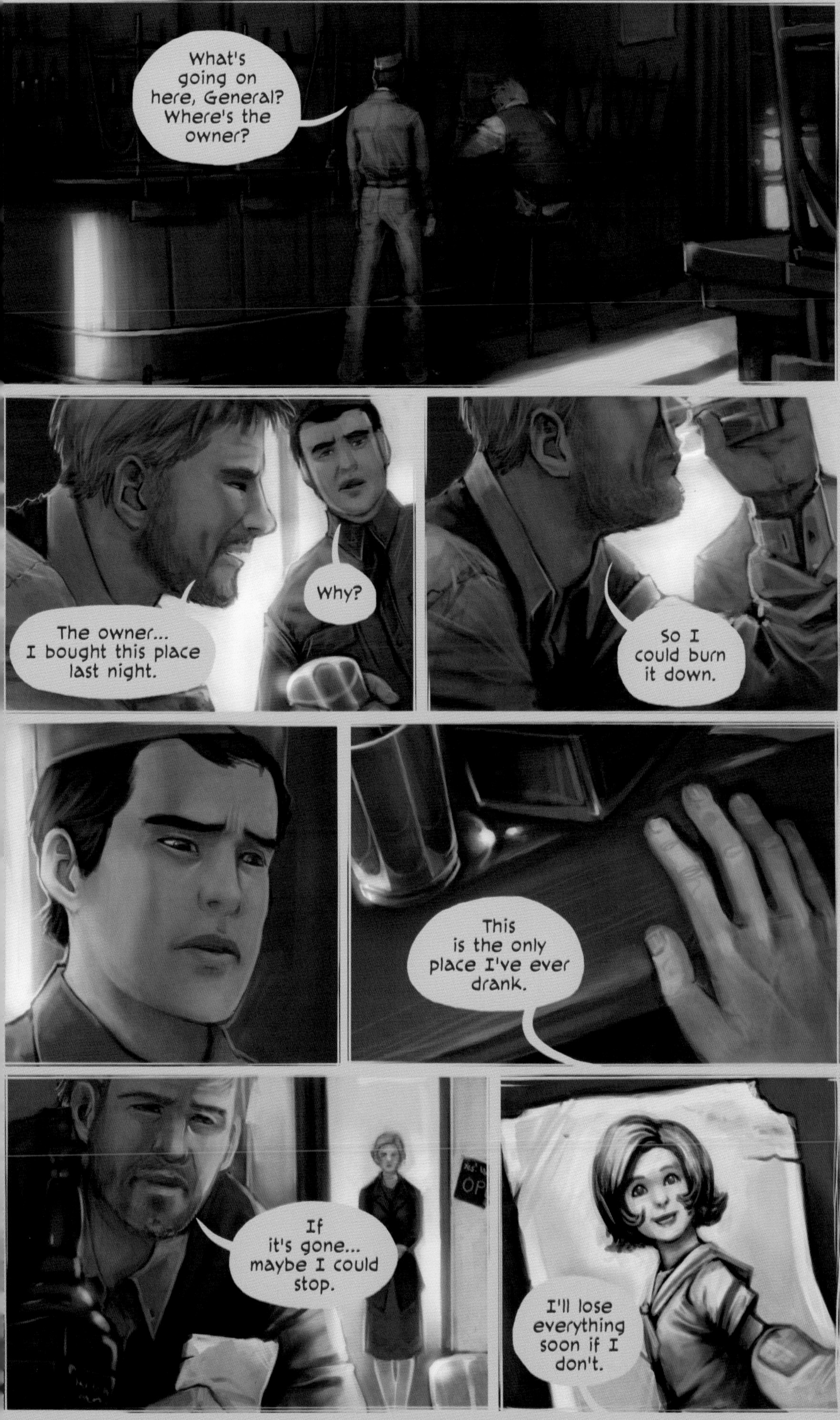
What's going on here, General? Where's the owner?
The owner... I bought this place last night.
Why?
So I could burn it down.
This is the only place I've ever drank.
If it's gone... maybe I could stop.
I'll lose everything soon if I don't.

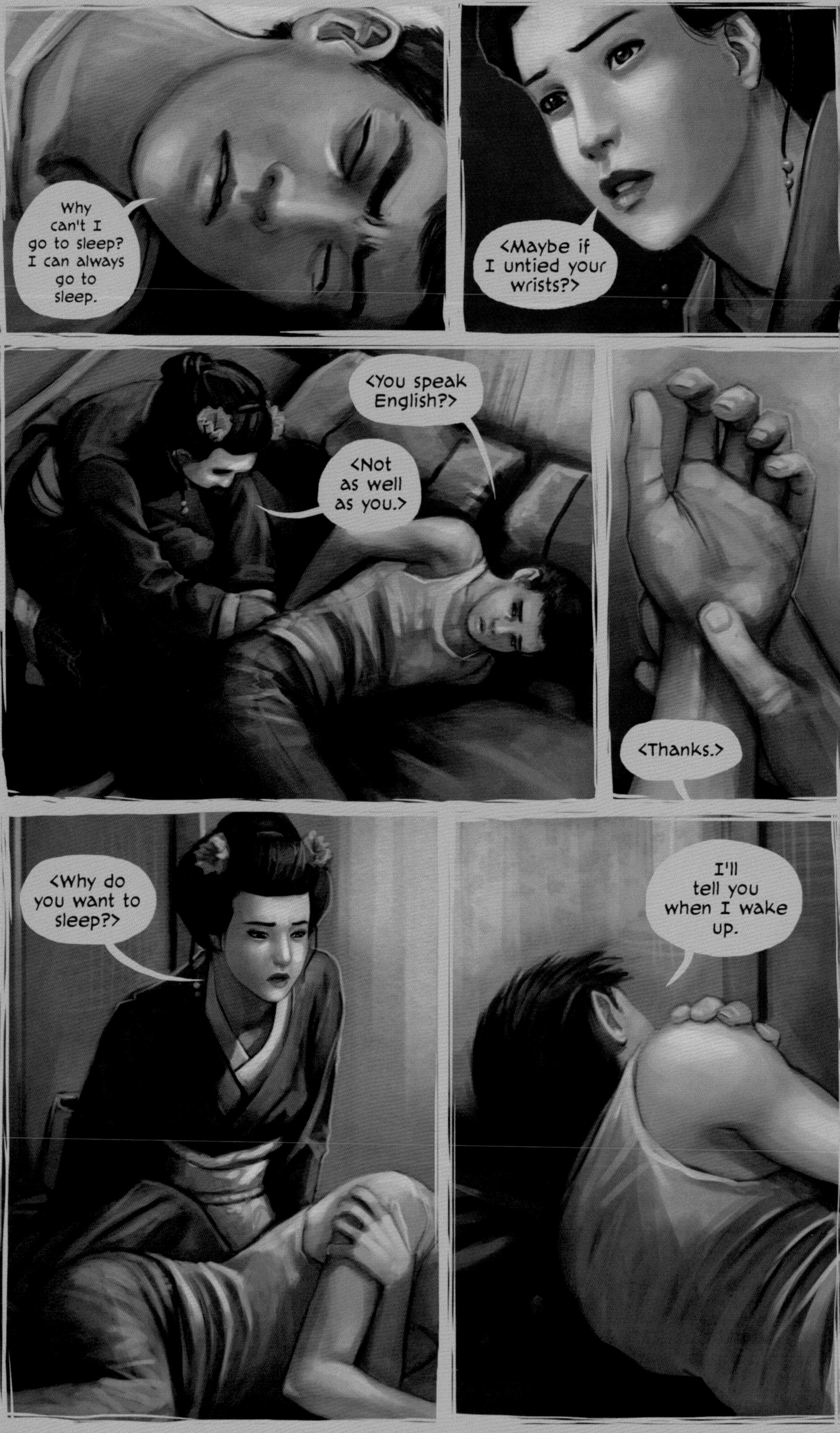
Why can't I go to sleep? I can always go to sleep.
<Maybe if I untied your wrists?>
<You speak English?>
<Not as well as you.>
<Thanks.>
<Why do you want to sleep?>
I'll tell you when I wake up.

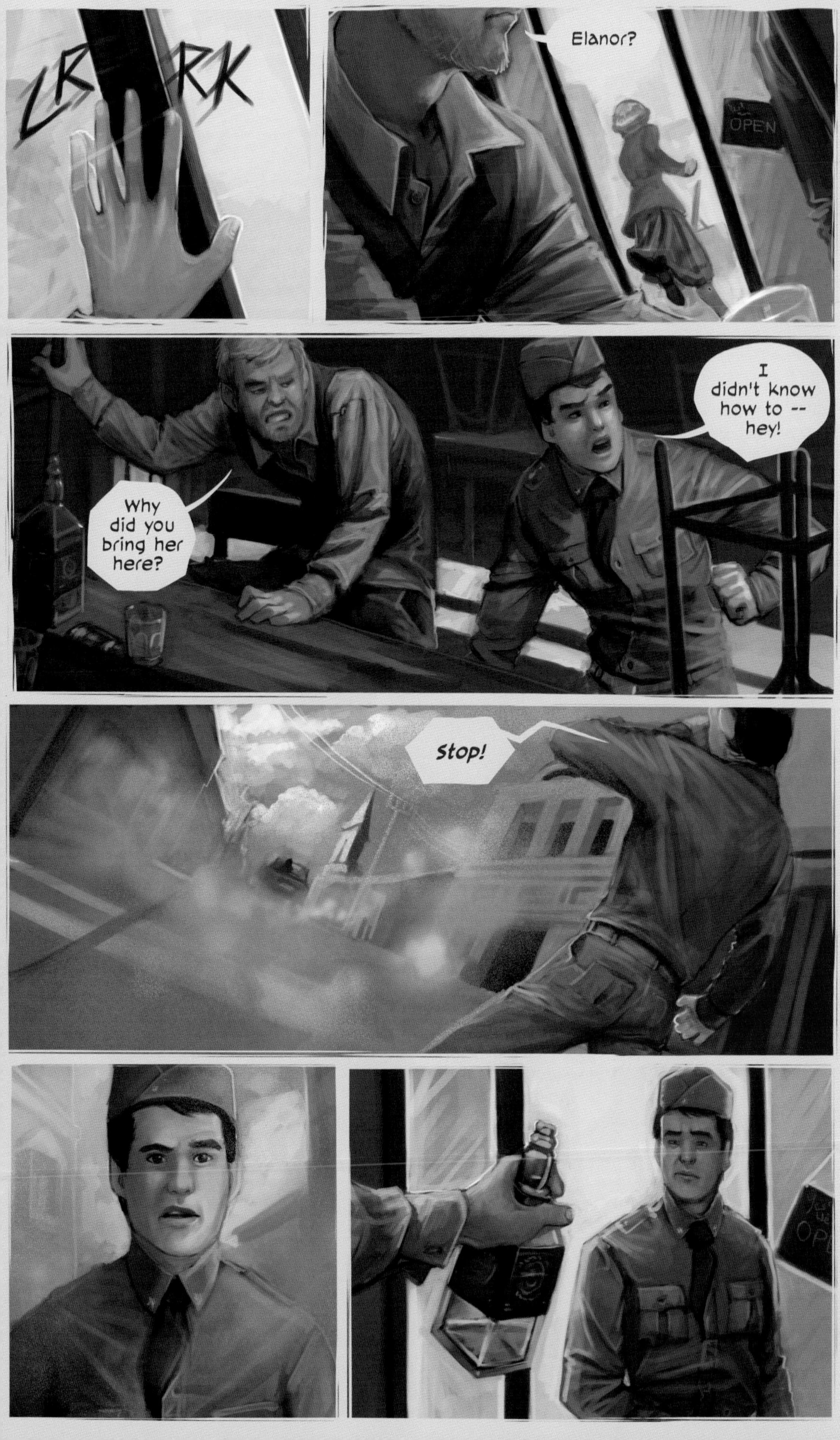

CRRK
Elanor?
OPEN
Why did you bring her here?
I didn't know how to -- hey!
Stop!

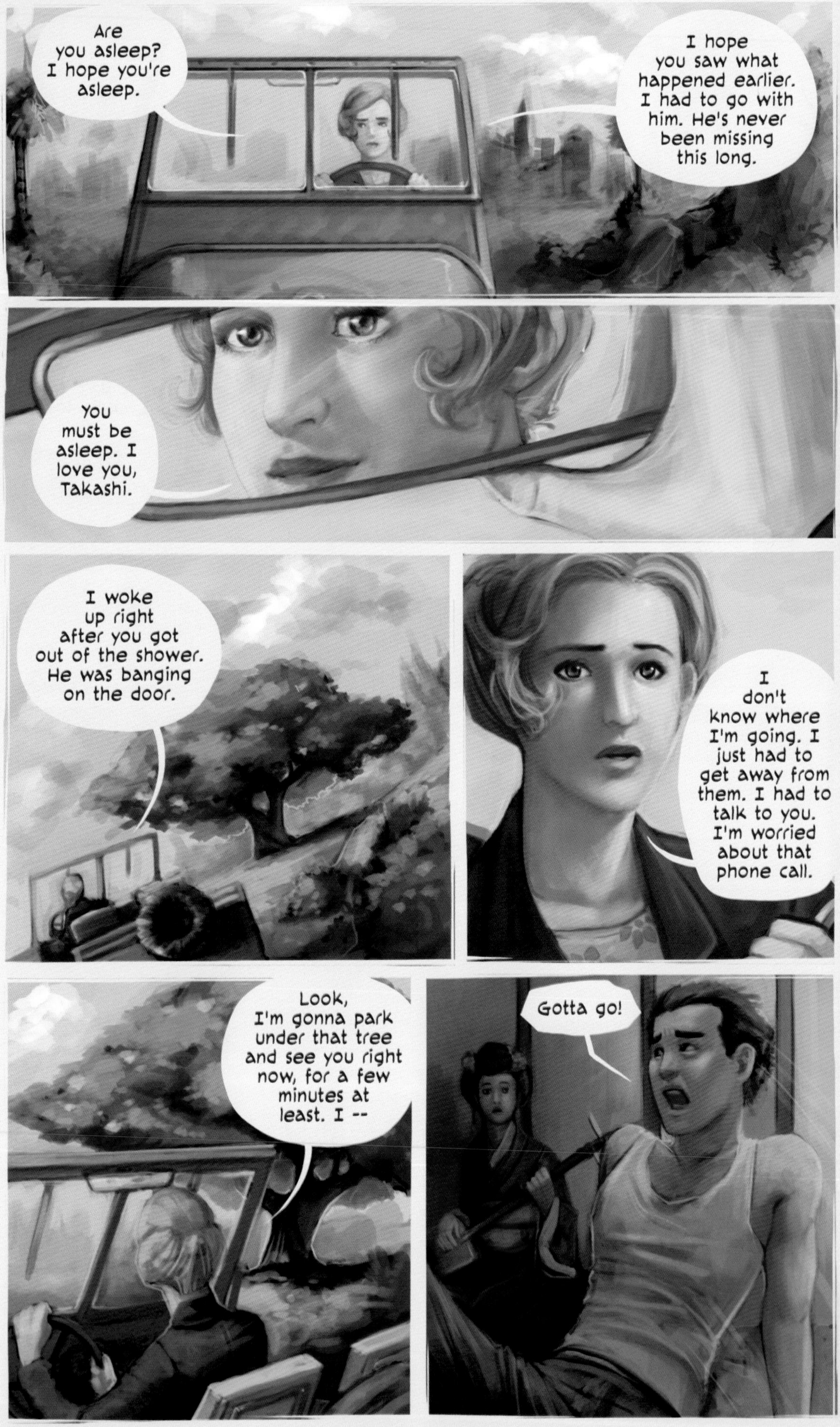
Are you asleep? I hope you're asleep.
I hope you saw what happened earlier. I had to go with him. He's never been missing this long.
You must be asleep. I love you, Takashi.
I woke up right after you got out of the shower. He was banging on the door.
I don't know where I'm going. I just had to get away from them. I had to talk to you. I'm worried about that phone call.
Look, I'm gonna park under that tree and see you right now, for a few minutes at least. I --
Gotta go!

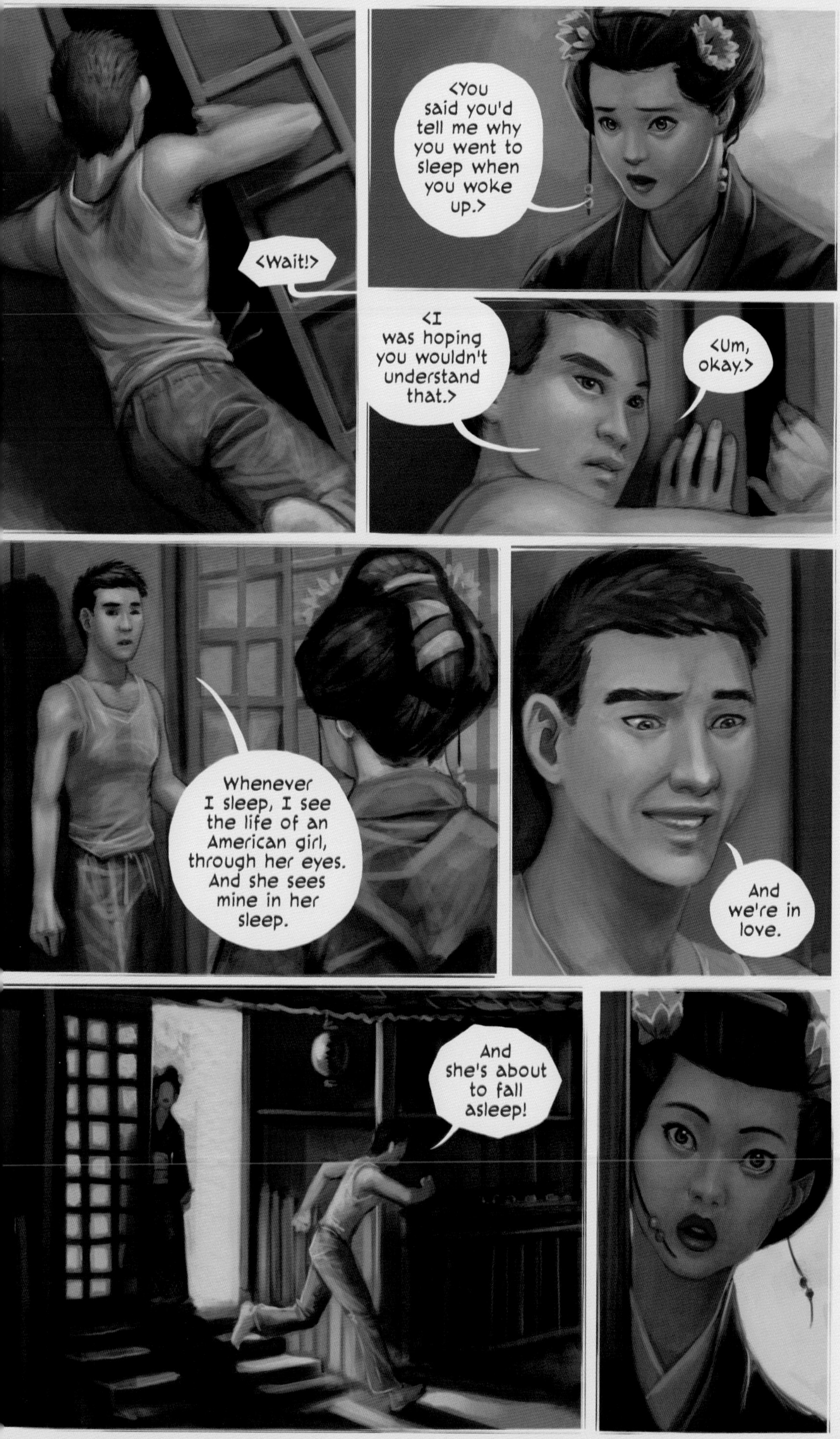
<Wait!>
<You said you'd tell me why you went to sleep when you woke up.>
<I was hoping you wouldn't understand that.>
<Um, okay.>
Whenever I sleep, I see the life of an American girl, through her eyes. And she sees mine in her sleep.
And we're in love.
And she's about to fall asleep!

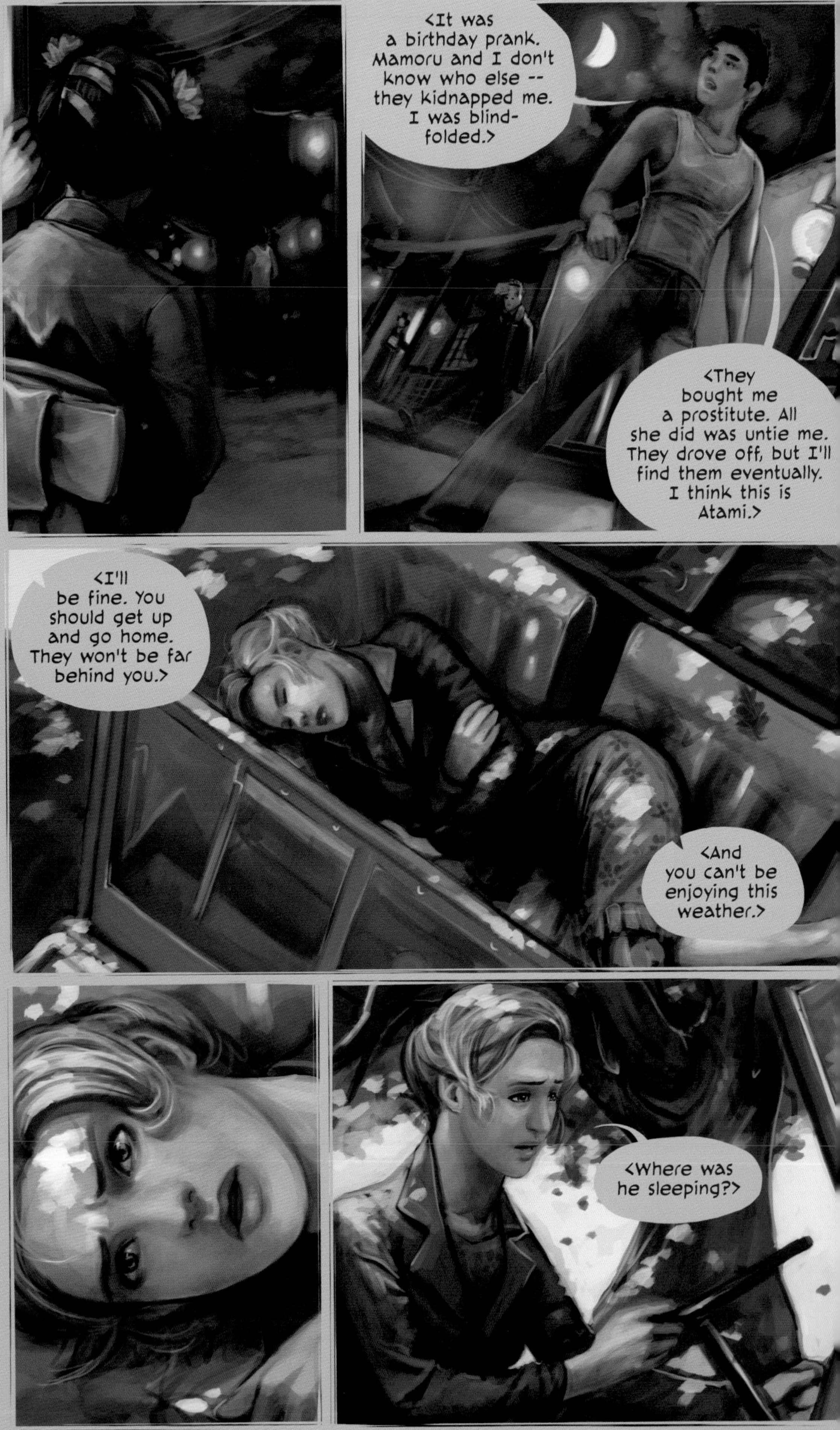
<It was a birthday prank. Mamoru and I don't know who else -- they kidnapped me. I was blind-folded.>
<They bought me a prostitute. All she did was untie me. They drove off, but I'll find them eventually. I think this is Atami.>
<I'll be fine. You should get up and go home. They won't be far behind you.>
<And you can't be enjoying this weather.>
<Where was he sleeping?>

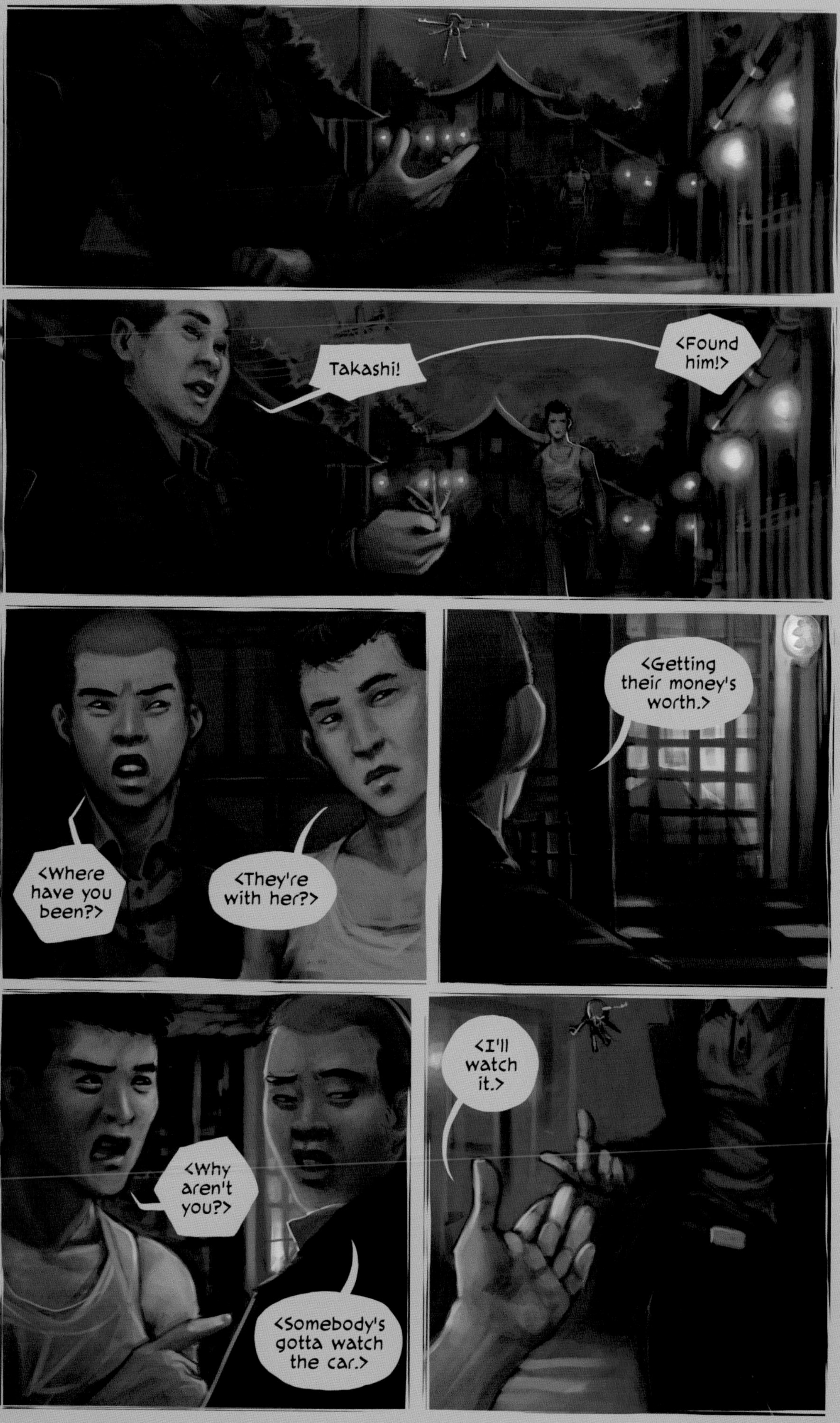
Takashi!
<Found him!>
<Where have you been?>
<They're with her?>
<Getting their money's worth.>
<Why aren't you?>
<Somebody's gotta watch the car.>
<I'll watch it.>

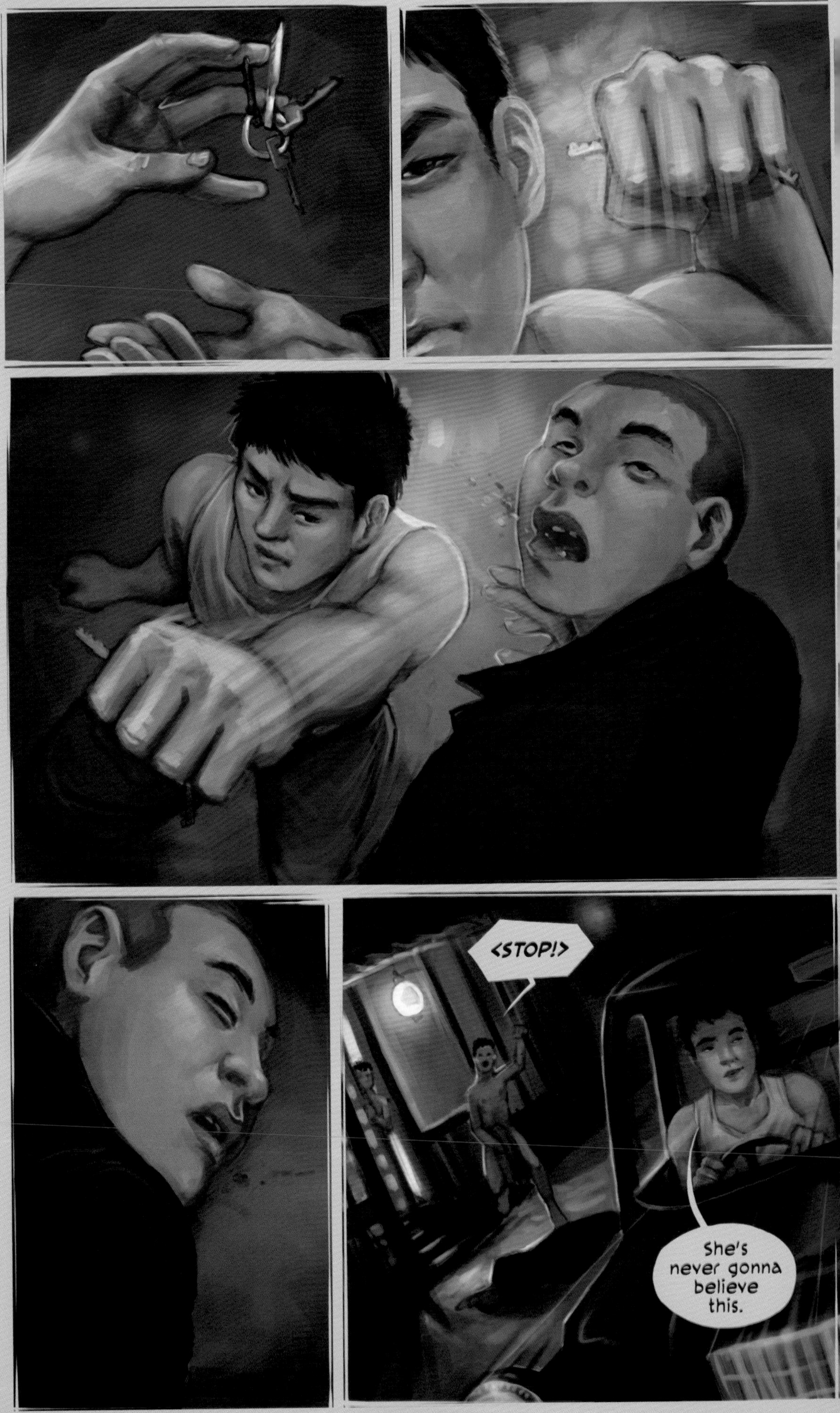
<STOP!>
She's never gonna believe this.

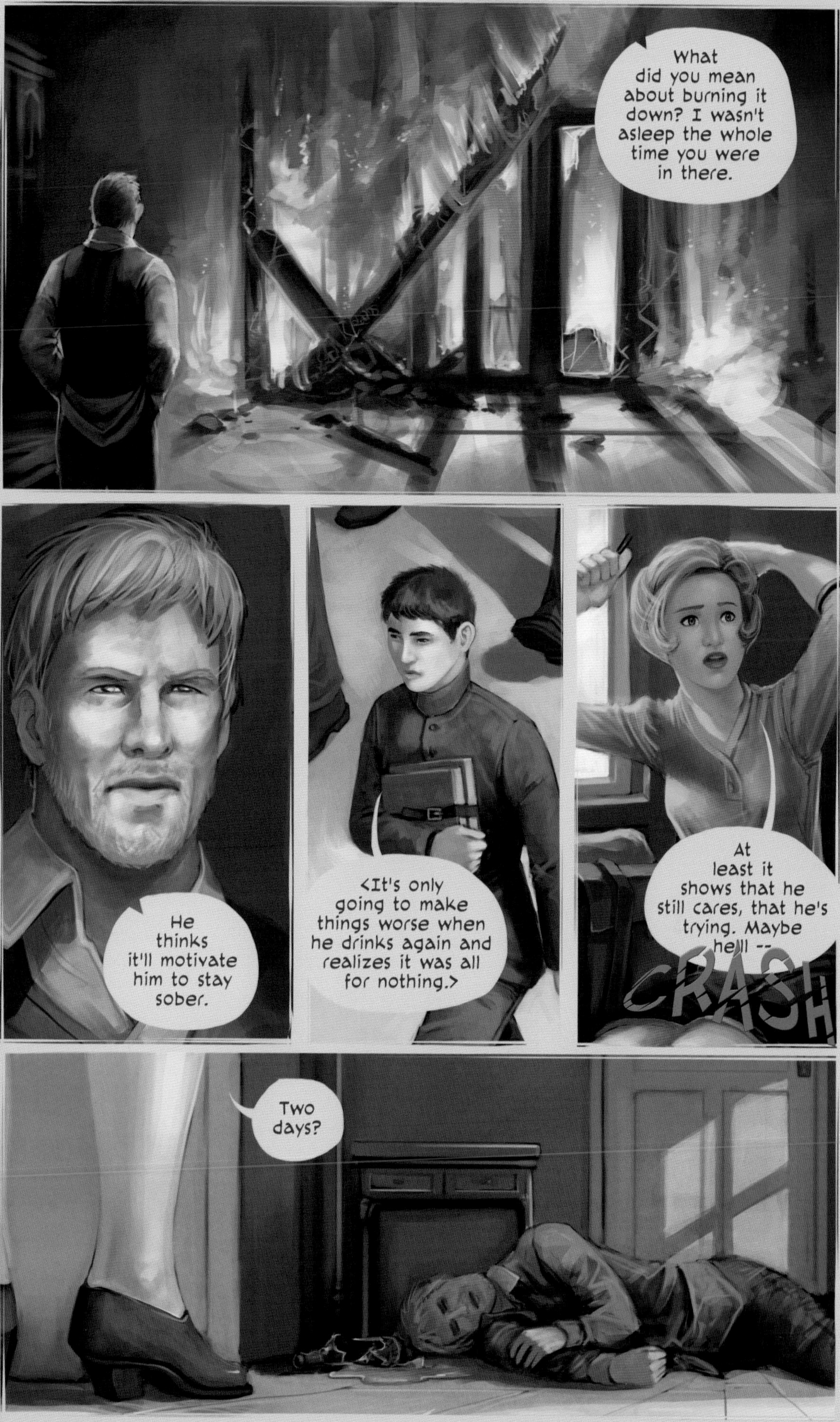
What did you mean about burning it down? I wasn't asleep the whole time you were in there.
He thinks it'll motivate him to stay sober.
<It's only going to make things worse when he drinks again and realizes it was all for nothing.>
At least it shows that he still cares, that he's trying. Maybe he'll --
CRASH
Two days?

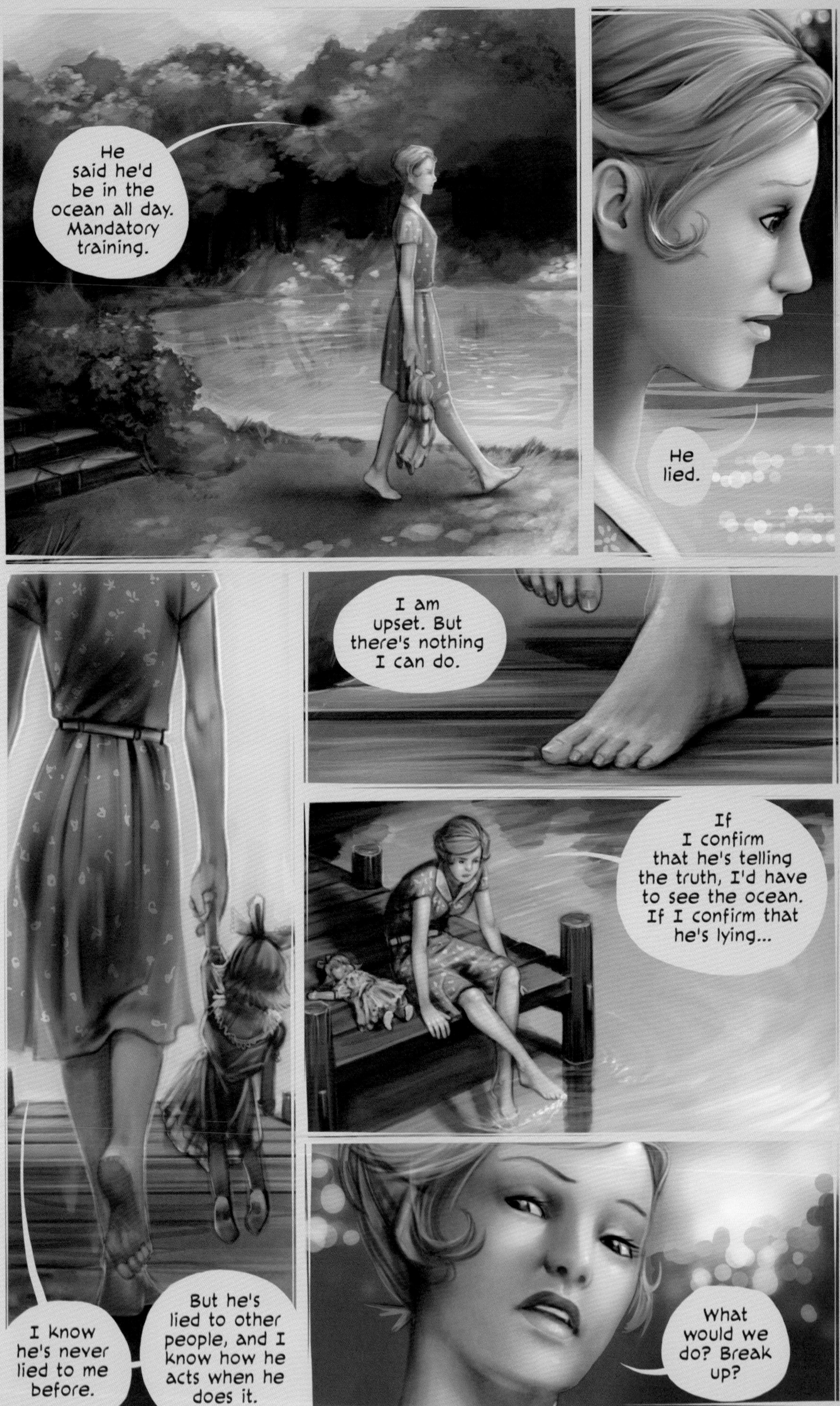
He said he'd be in the ocean all day. Mandatory training.
He lied.
I know he's never lied to me before.
But he's lied to other people, and I know how he acts when he does it.
I am upset. But there's nothing I can do.
If I confirm that he's telling the truth, I'd have to see the ocean. If I confirm that he's lying...
What would we do? Break up?

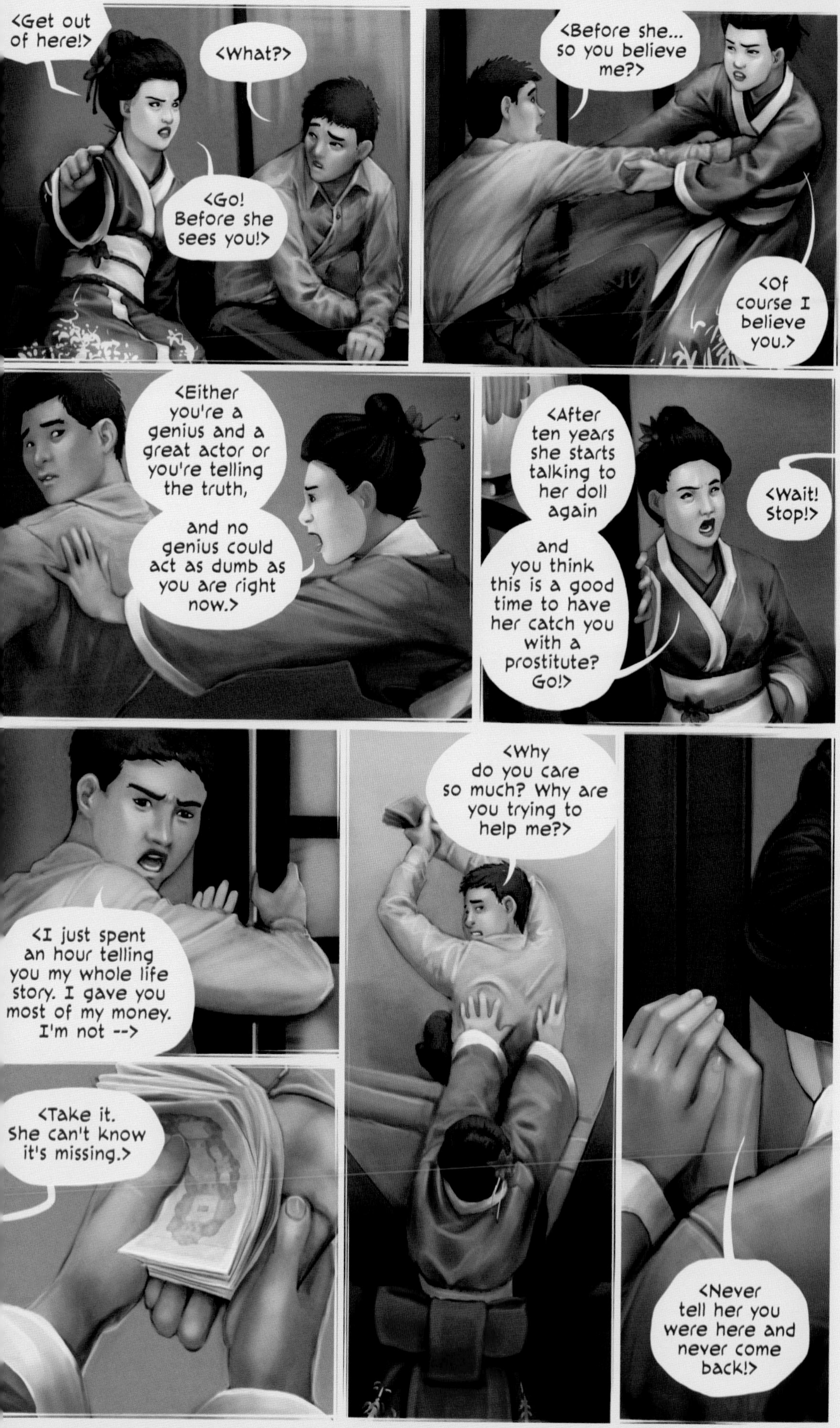
<Get out of here!>
<What?>
<Go! Before she sees you!>
<Before she... so you believe me?>
<Of course I believe you.>
<Either you're a genius and a great actor or you're telling the truth,
and no genius could act as dumb as you are right now.>
<After ten years she starts talking to her doll again
and you think this is a good time to have her catch you with a prostitute? Go!>
<Wait! Stop!>
<I just spent an hour telling you my whole life story. I gave you most of my money. I'm not -->
<Take it. She can't know it's missing.>
<Why do you care so much? Why are you trying to help me?>
<Never tell her you were here and never come back!>

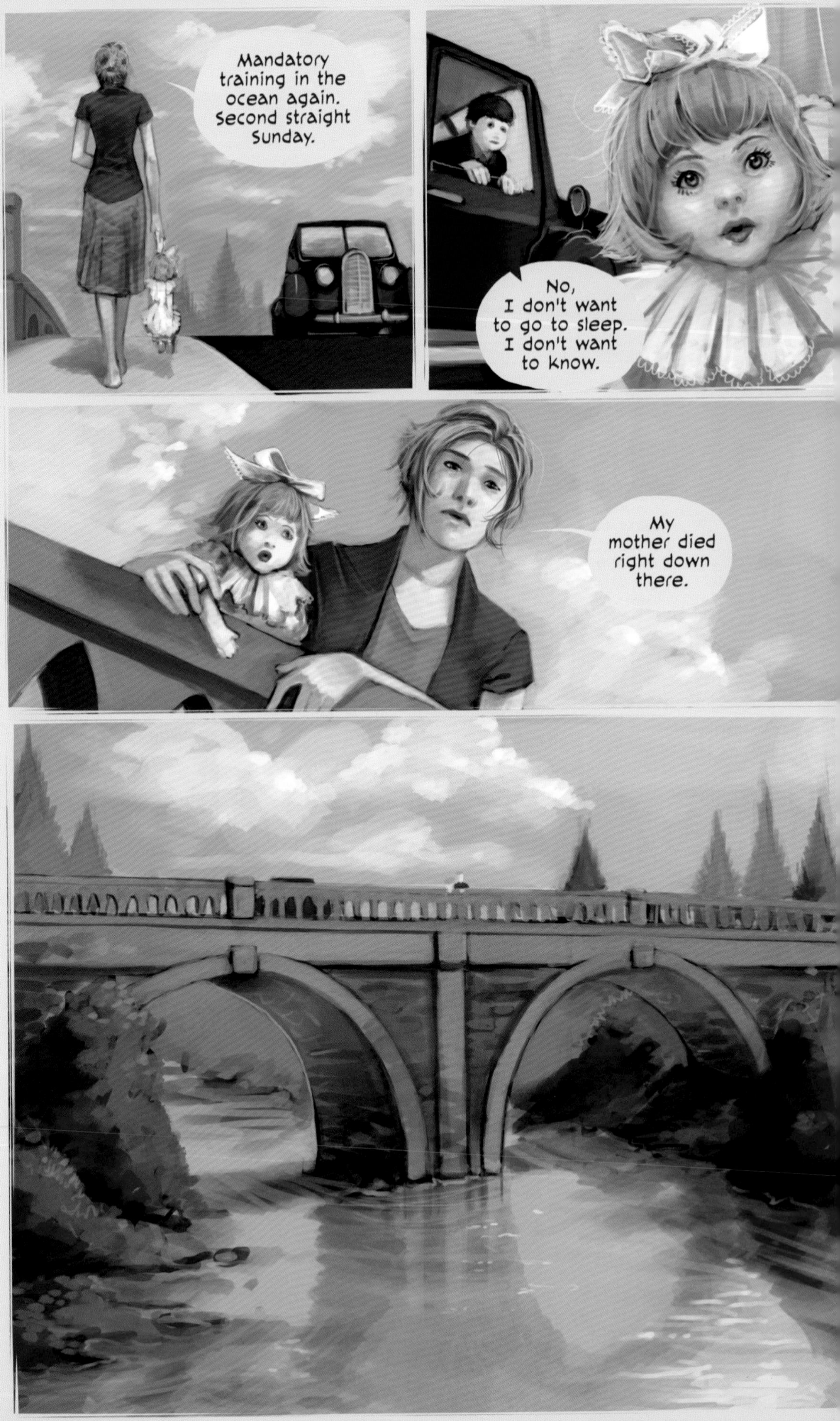
Mandatory training in the ocean again. Second straight Sunday.
No, I don't want to go to sleep. I don't want to know.
My mother died right down there.

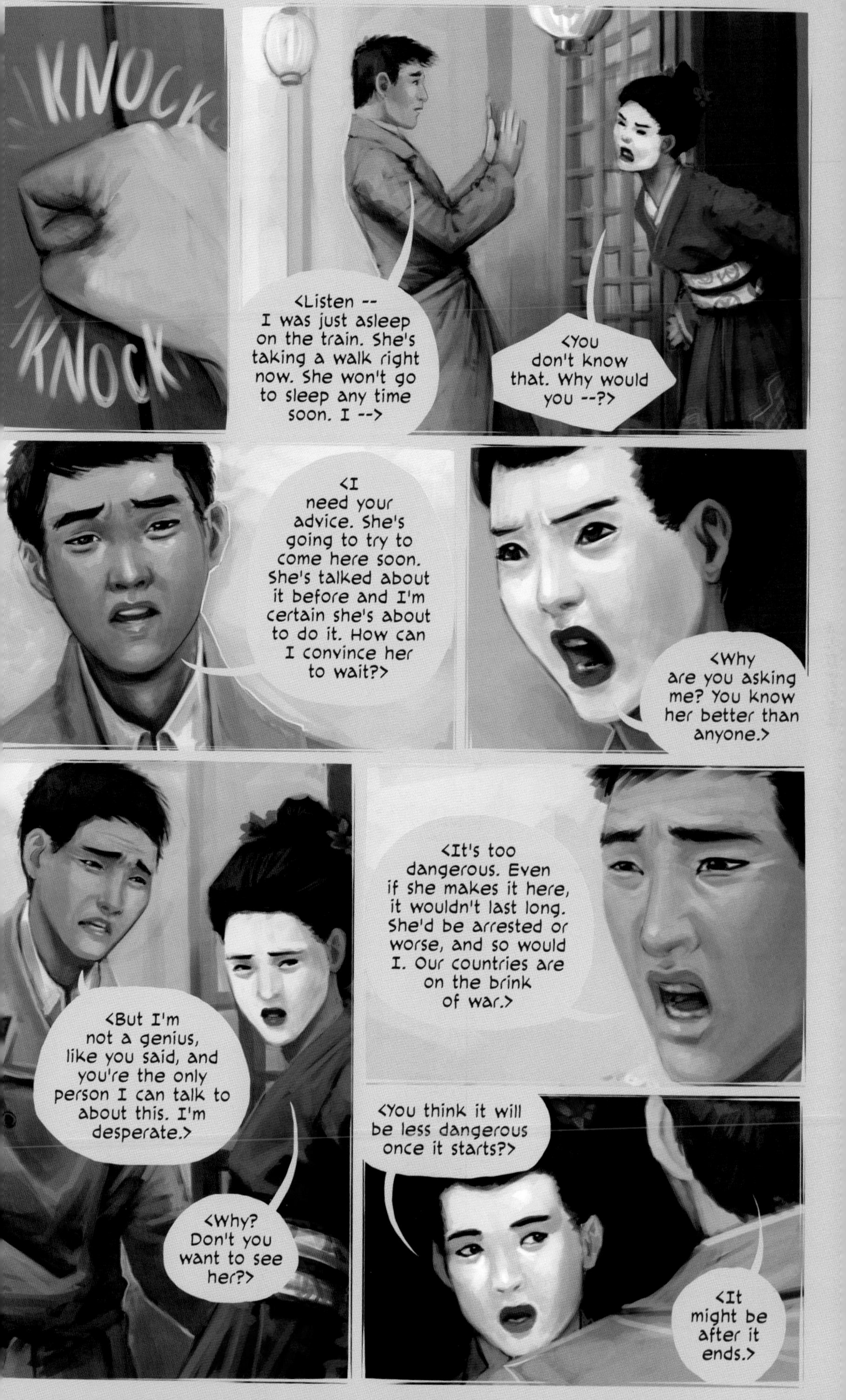
KNOCK
KNOCK
<Listen -- I was just asleep on the train. She's taking a walk right now. She won't go to sleep any time soon. I -->
<You don't know that. Why would you --?>
<I need your advice. She's going to try to come here soon. She's talked about it before and I'm certain she's about to do it. How can I convince her to wait?>
<Why are you asking me? You know her better than anyone.>
<But I'm not a genius, like you said, and you're the only person I can talk to about this. I'm desperate.>
<Why? Don't you want to see her?>
<It's too dangerous. Even if she makes it here, it wouldn't last long. She'd be arrested or worse, and so would I. Our countries are on the brink of war.>
<You think it will be less dangerous once it starts?>
<It might be after it ends.>

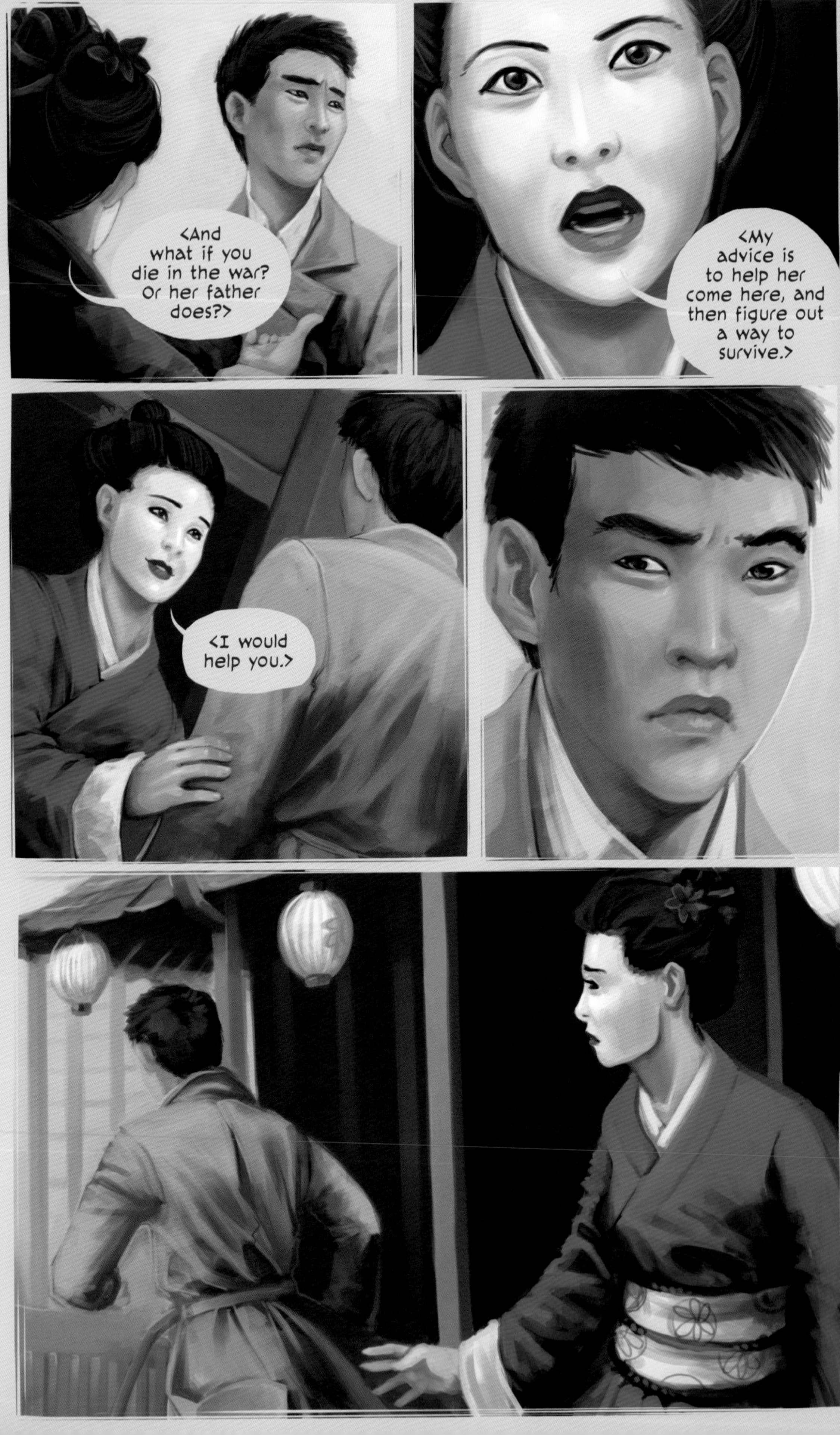
<And what if you die in the war? Or her father does?>
<My advice is to help her come here, and then figure out a way to survive.>
<I would help you.>

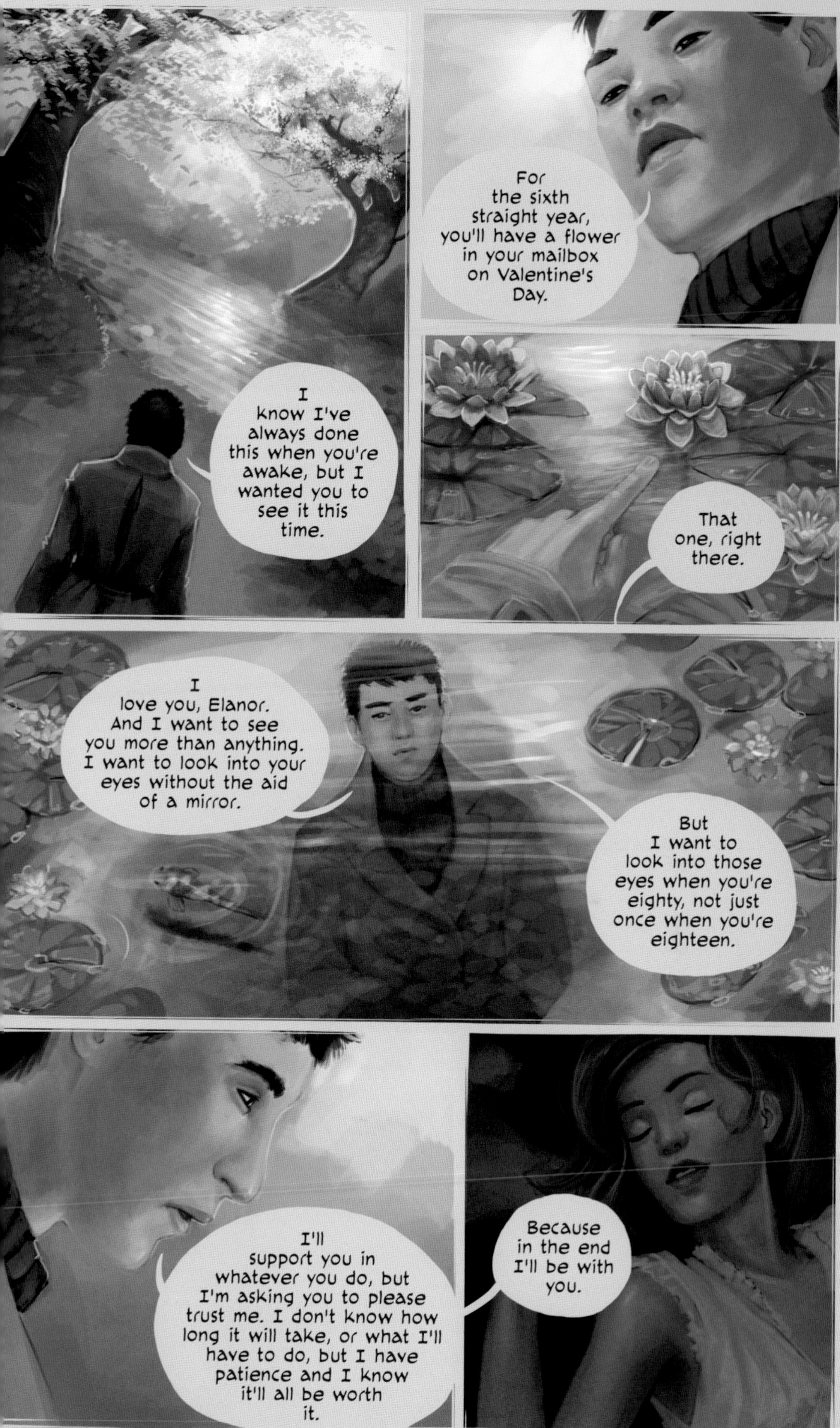

I know I've always done this when you're awake, but I wanted you to see it this time.
For the sixth straight year, you'll have a flower in your mailbox on Valentine's Day.
That one, right there.
I love you, Elanor. And I want to see you more than anything. I want to look into your eyes without the aid of a mirror.
But I want to look into those eyes when you're eighty, not just once when you're eighteen.
I'll support you in whatever you do, but I'm asking you to please trust me. I don't know how long it will take, or what I'll have to do, but I have patience and I know it'll all be worth it.
Because in the end I'll be with you.

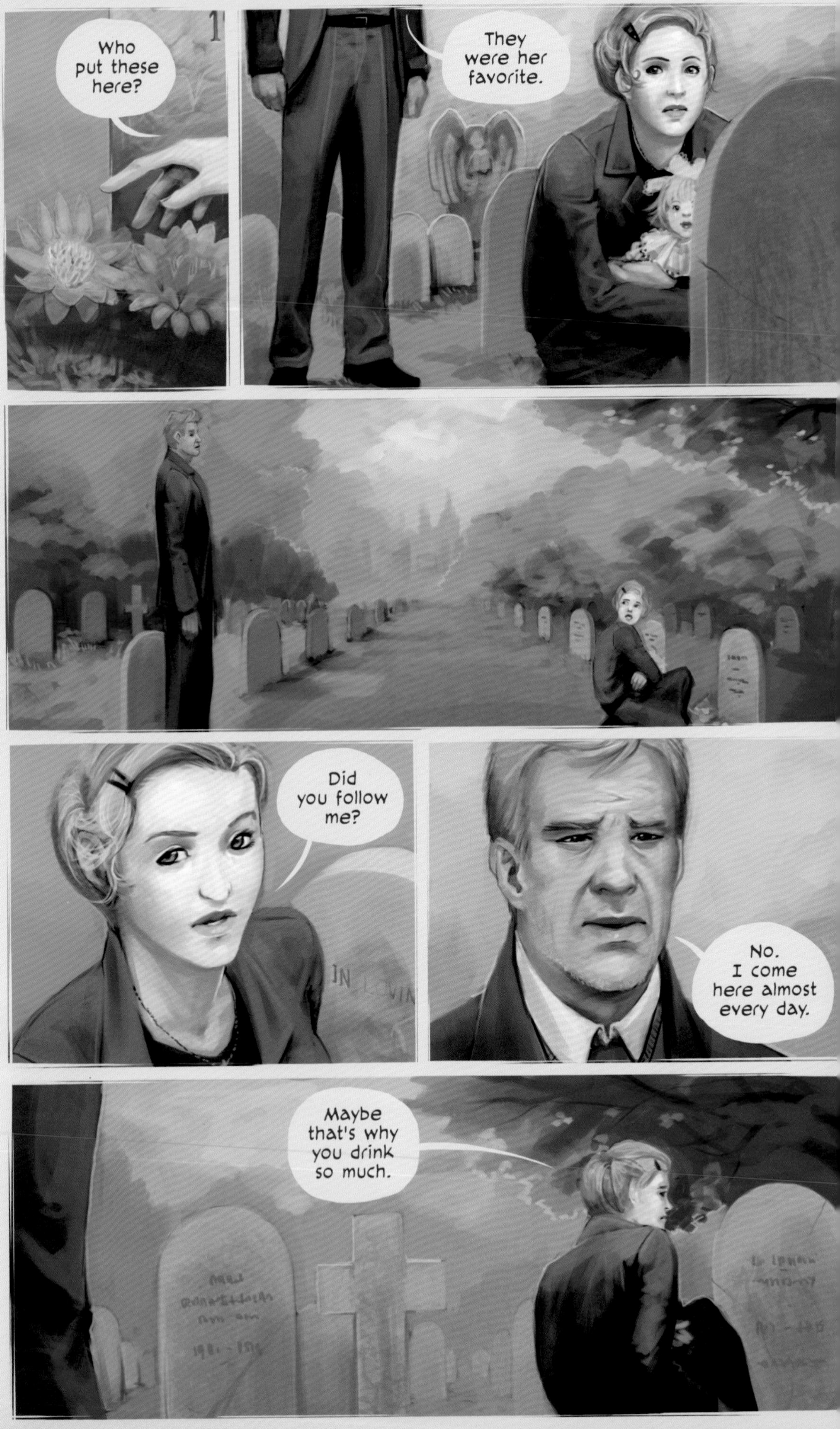
Who put these here?
They were her favorite.
Did you follow me?
No. I come here almost every day.
Maybe that's why you drink so much.

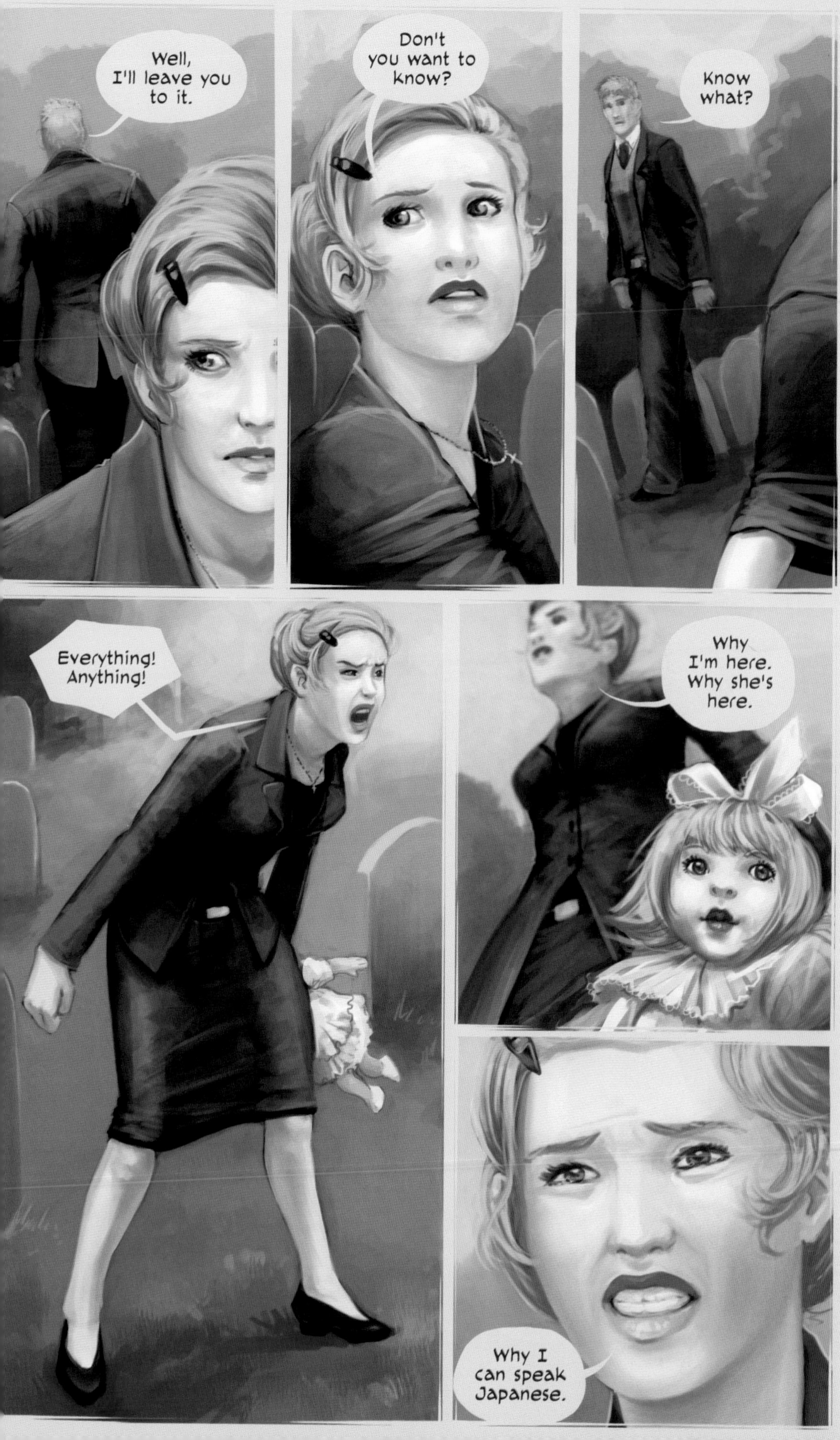
Well, I'll leave you to it.
Don't you want to know?
Know what?
Everything! Anything!
Why I'm here. Why she's here.
Why I can speak Japanese.

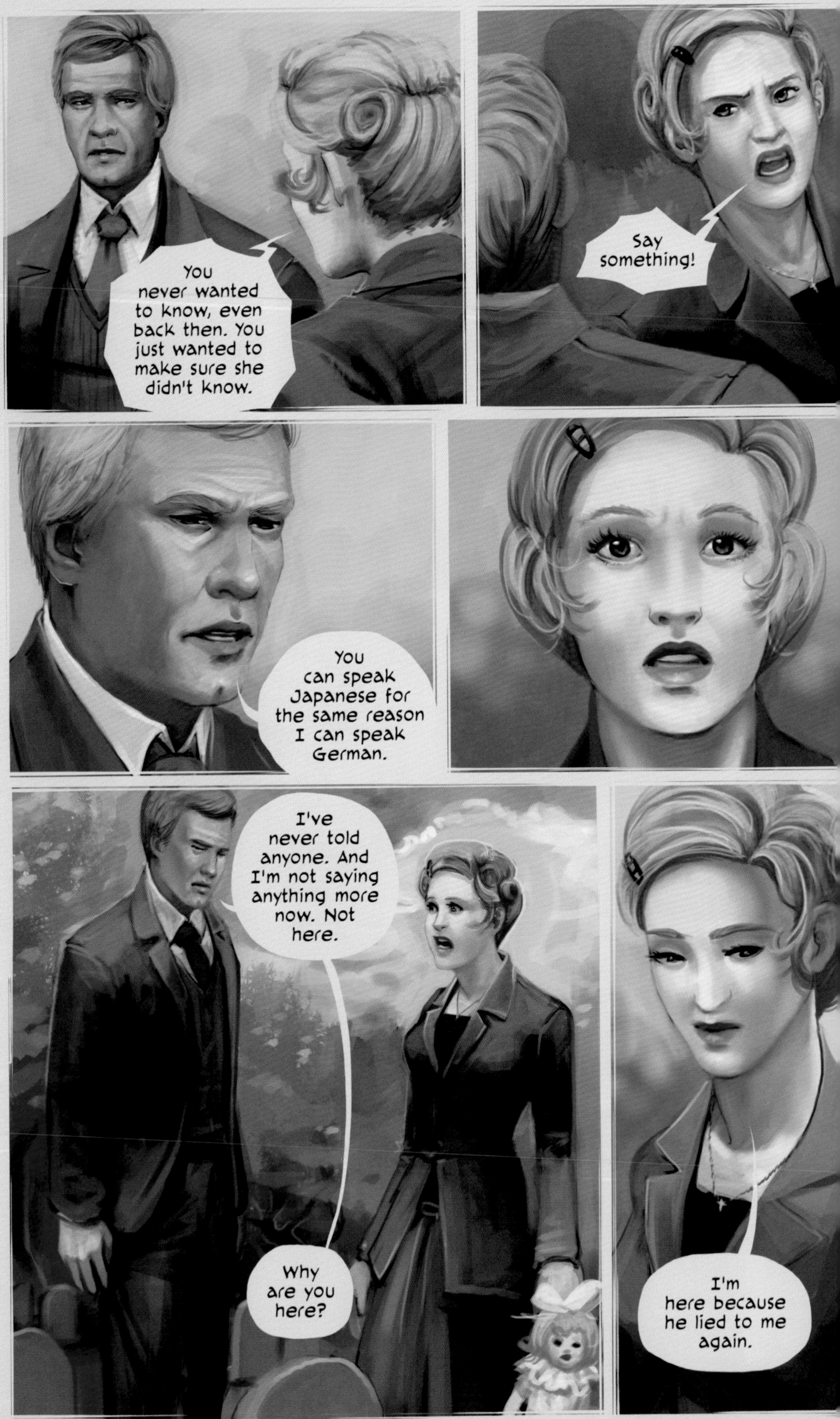
You never wanted to know, even back then. You just wanted to make sure she didn't know.
Say something!
You can speak Japanese for the same reason I can speak German.
I've never told anyone. And I'm not saying anything more now. Not here.
Why are you here?
I'm here because he lied to me again.

<You're not going to marry me, are you?>

<Why do you say that?>

<I've gone through this before. You're acting the same way he did.>

<He died last week in the war. Lost at sea.>

<It's for the best, since his family can't afford a proper funeral now.>

<Not after what my father did to them.>

<I'm sorry to interrupt, but you have a telephone call.>

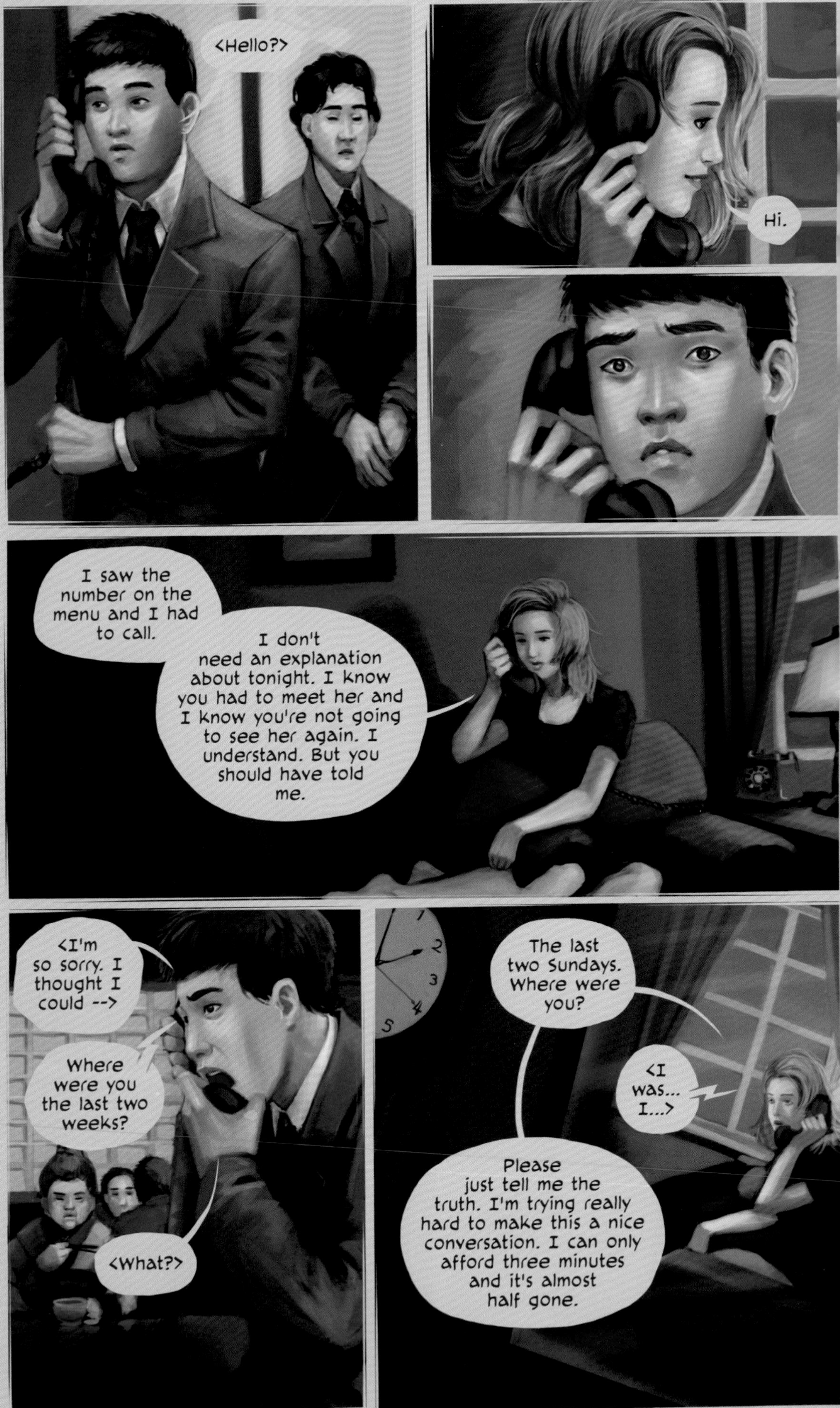
<Hello?>
Hi.
I saw the number on the menu and I had to call.
I don't need an explanation about tonight. I know you had to meet her and I know you're not going to see her again. I understand. But you should have told me.
<I'm so sorry. I thought I could -->
Where were you the last two weeks?
<What?>
The last two Sundays. Where were you?
<I was... I...>
Please just tell me the truth. I'm trying really hard to make this a nice conversation. I can only afford three minutes and it's almost half gone.

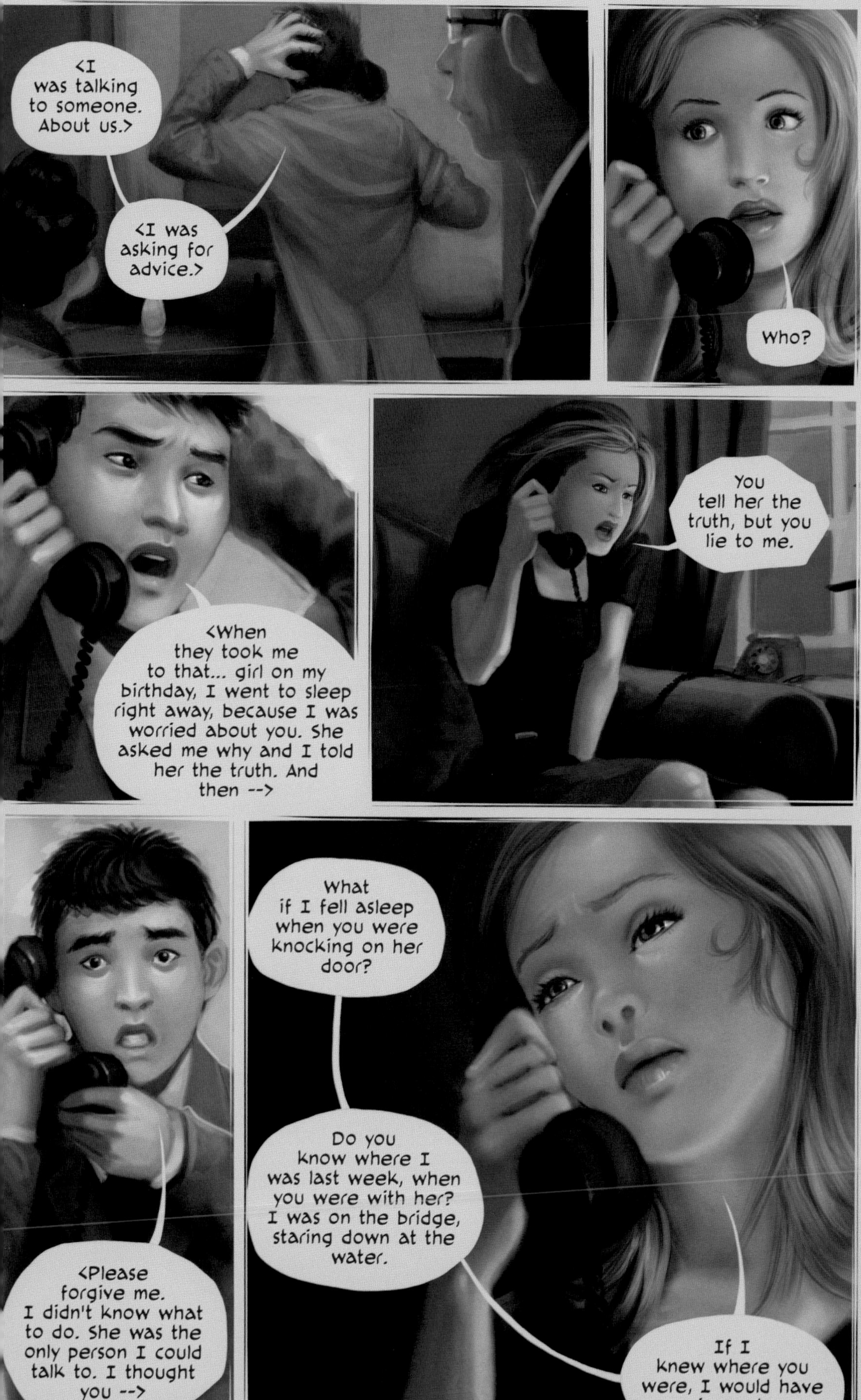
<I was talking to someone. About us.>
<I was asking for advice.>
Who?
<When they took me to that... girl on my birthday, I went to sleep right away, because I was worried about you. She asked me why and I told her the truth. And then -->
You tell her the truth, but you lie to me.
<Please forgive me. I didn't know what to do. She was the only person I could talk to. I thought you -->
What if I fell asleep when you were knocking on her door?
Do you know where I was last week, when you were with her? I was on the bridge, staring down at the water.
If I knew where you were, I would have jumped.

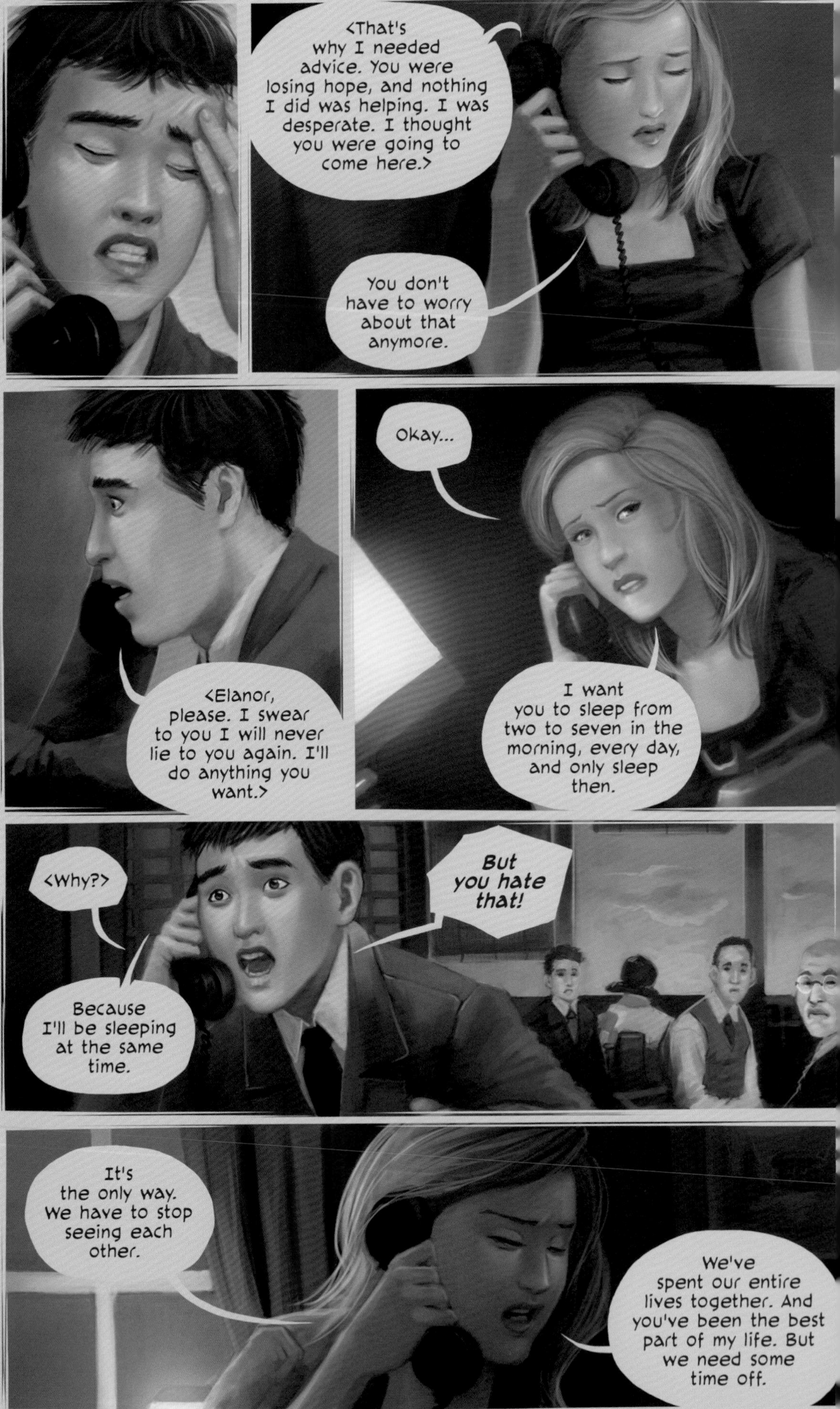
<That's why I needed advice. You were losing hope, and nothing I did was helping. I was desperate. I thought you were going to come here.>
You don't have to worry about that anymore.
<Elanor, please. I swear to you I will never lie to you again. I'll do anything you want.>
Okay...
I want you to sleep from two to seven in the morning, every day, and only sleep then.
<Why?>
Because I'll be sleeping at the same time.
But you hate that!
It's the only way. We have to stop seeing each other.
We've spent our entire lives together. And you've been the best part of my life. But we need some time off.

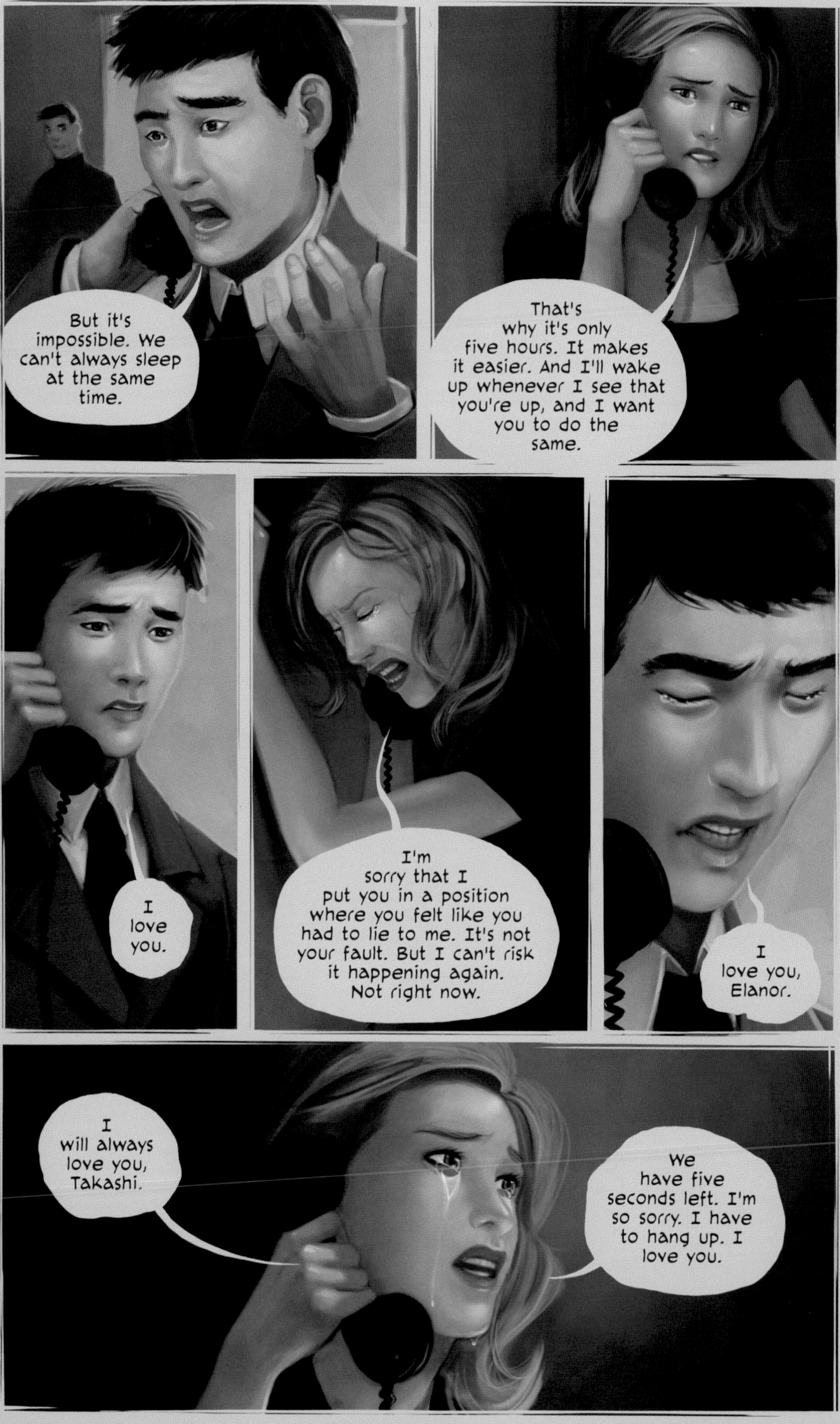
But it's impossible. We can't always sleep at the same time.
That's why it's only five hours. It makes it easier. And I'll wake up whenever I see that you're up, and I want you to do the same.
I love you.
I'm sorry that I put you in a position where you felt like you had to lie to me. It's not your fault. But I can't risk it happening again. Not right now.
I love you, Elanor.
I will always love you, Takashi.
We have five seconds left. I'm so sorry. I have to hang up. I love you.

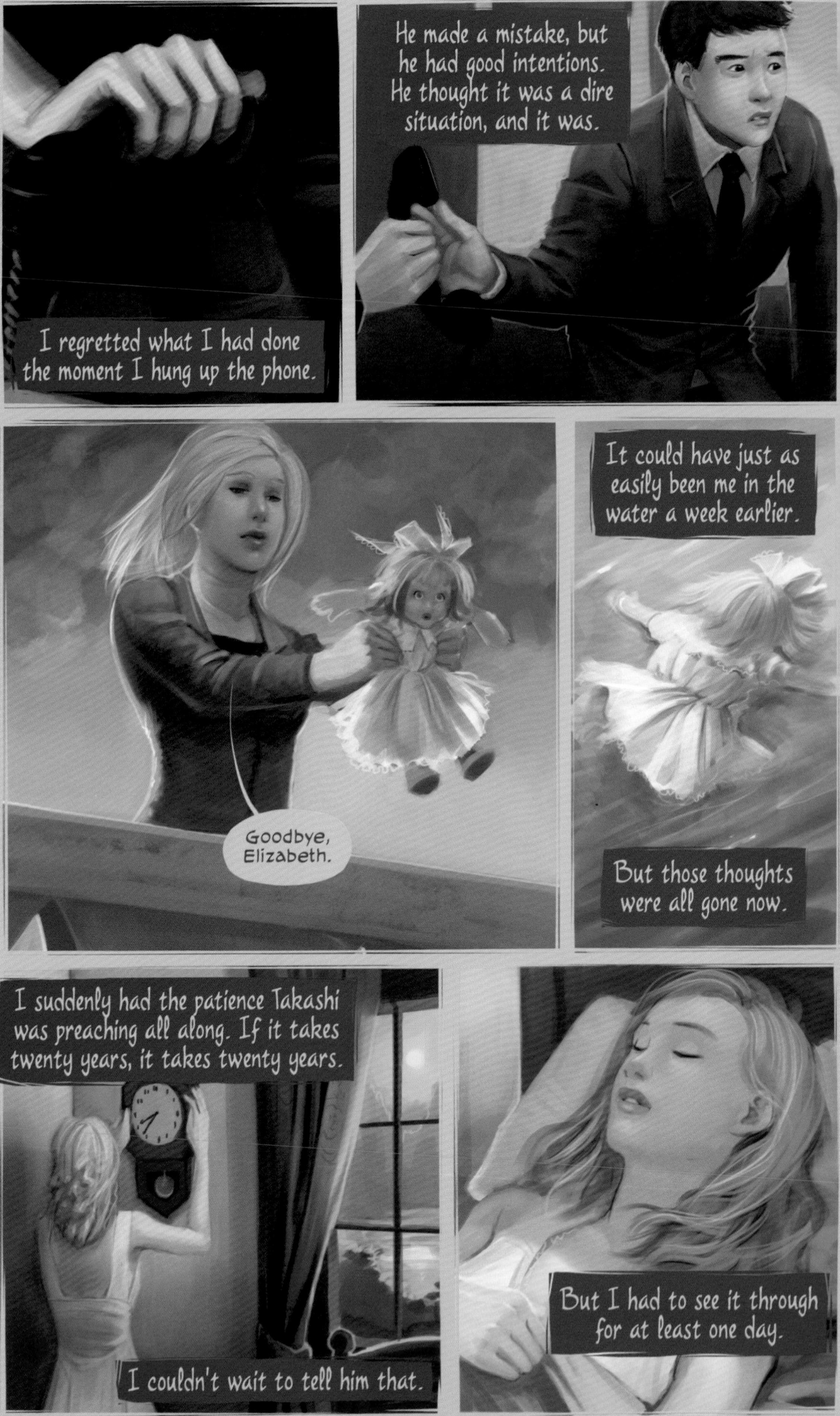
I regretted what I had done the moment I hung up the phone.
He made a mistake, but he had good intentions. He thought it was a dire situation, and it was.
Goodbye, Elizabeth.
It could have just as easily been me in the water a week earlier.
But those thoughts were all gone now.
I suddenly had the patience Takashi was preaching all along. If it takes twenty years, it takes twenty years.
I couldn't wait to tell him that.
But I had to see it through for at least one day.

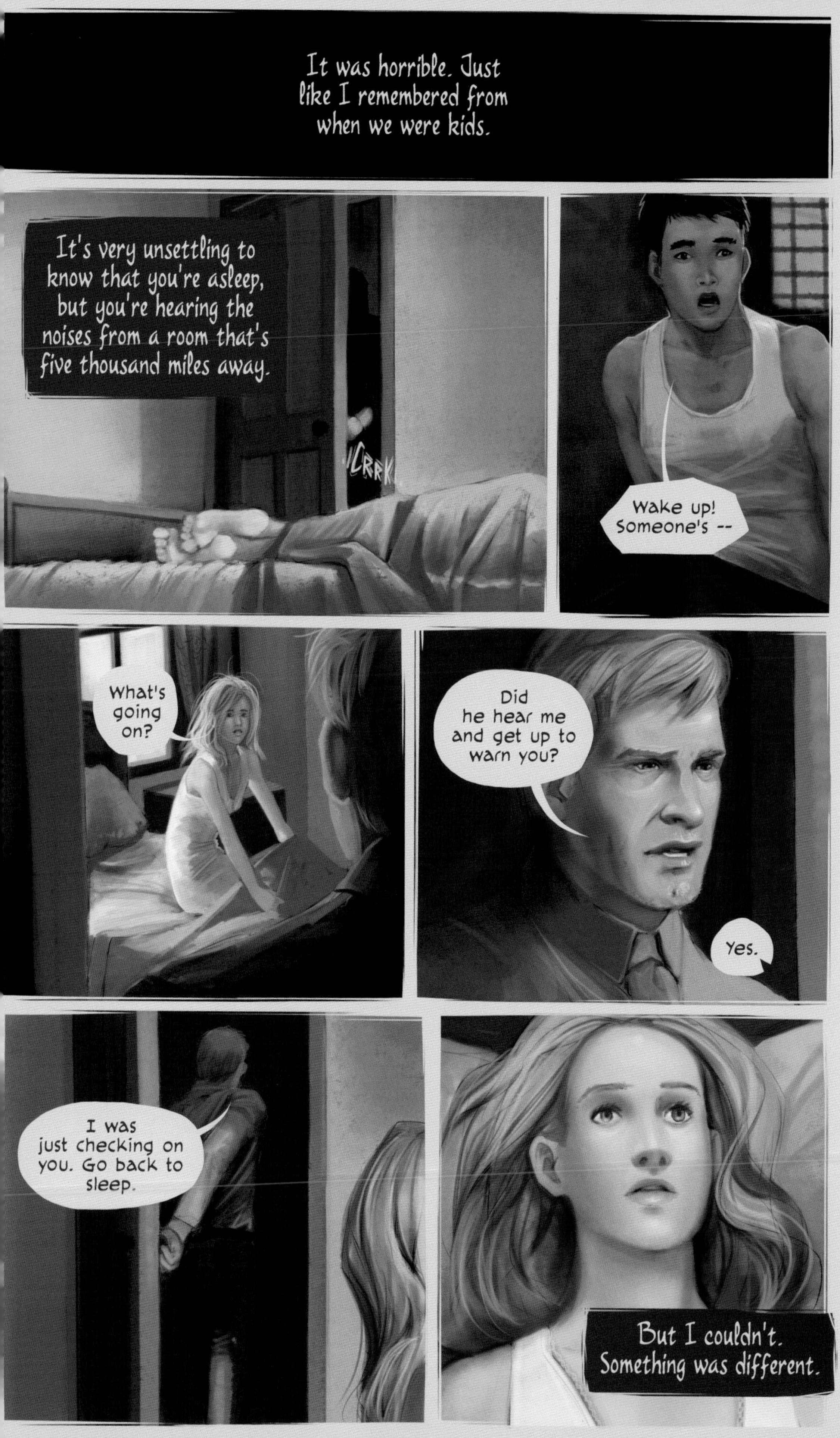
It was horrible. Just like I remembered from when we were kids.
It's very unsettling to know that you're asleep, but you're hearing the noises from a room that's five thousand miles away.
CRRK
Wake up! Someone's --
What's going on?
Did he hear me and get up to warn you?
Yes.
I was just checking on you. Go back to sleep.
But I couldn't. Something was different.

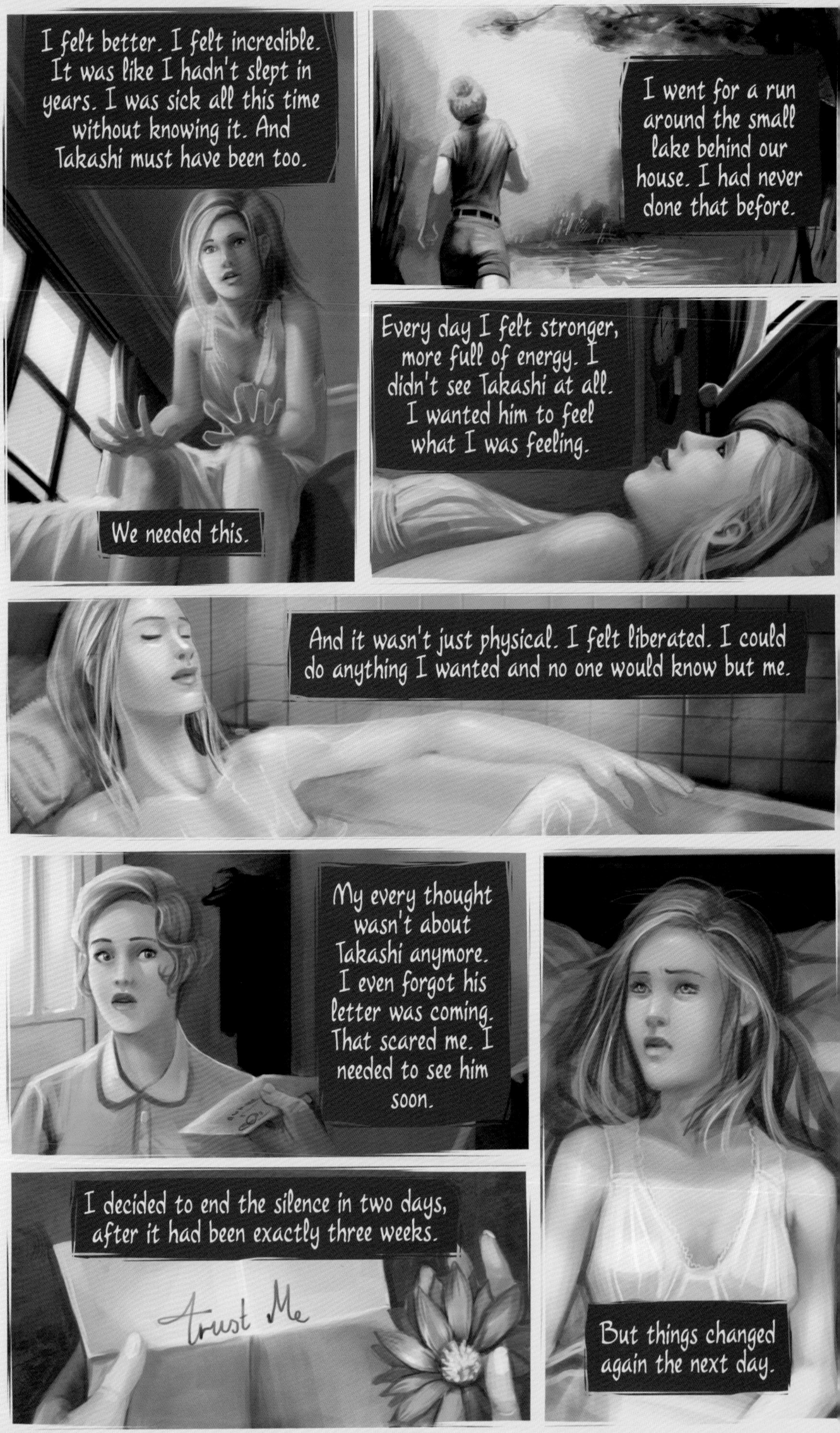
I felt better. I felt incredible. It was like I hadn't slept in years. I was sick all this time without knowing it. And Takashi must have been too.
We needed this.
I went for a run around the small lake behind our house. I had never done that before.
Every day I felt stronger, more full of energy. I didn't see Takashi at all. I wanted him to feel what I was feeling.
And it wasn't just physical. I felt liberated. I could do anything I wanted and no one would know but me.
My every thought wasn't about Takashi anymore. I even forgot his letter was coming. That scared me. I needed to see him soon.
I decided to end the silence in two days, after it had been exactly three weeks.
Trust Me
But things changed again the next day.

I was sick. I could barely sit up.

I didn't want Takashi to see me like this.

And I couldn't let Takashi watch me die. I had put him through too much already.

I was worse the next day, and every day after that. The doctors didn't know what was wrong.

I felt like the extra healing power of the synchronized sleep was the only thing keeping me alive.

In the summer he started sleeping with the hair I sent him years ago. I loved him more than ever.

I have to go to sleep now.

I stopped keeping track of the days, the months. By the time I was given the last rites, I couldn't have told you what year it was with any certainty.

I'm sorry.

All I cared about was protecting Takashi from the truth. I had to be asleep by nine.

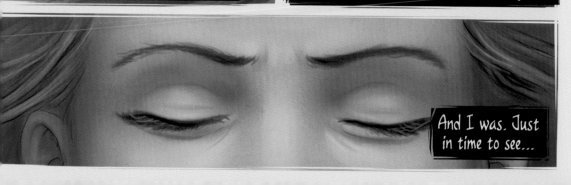

And I was. Just in time to see...

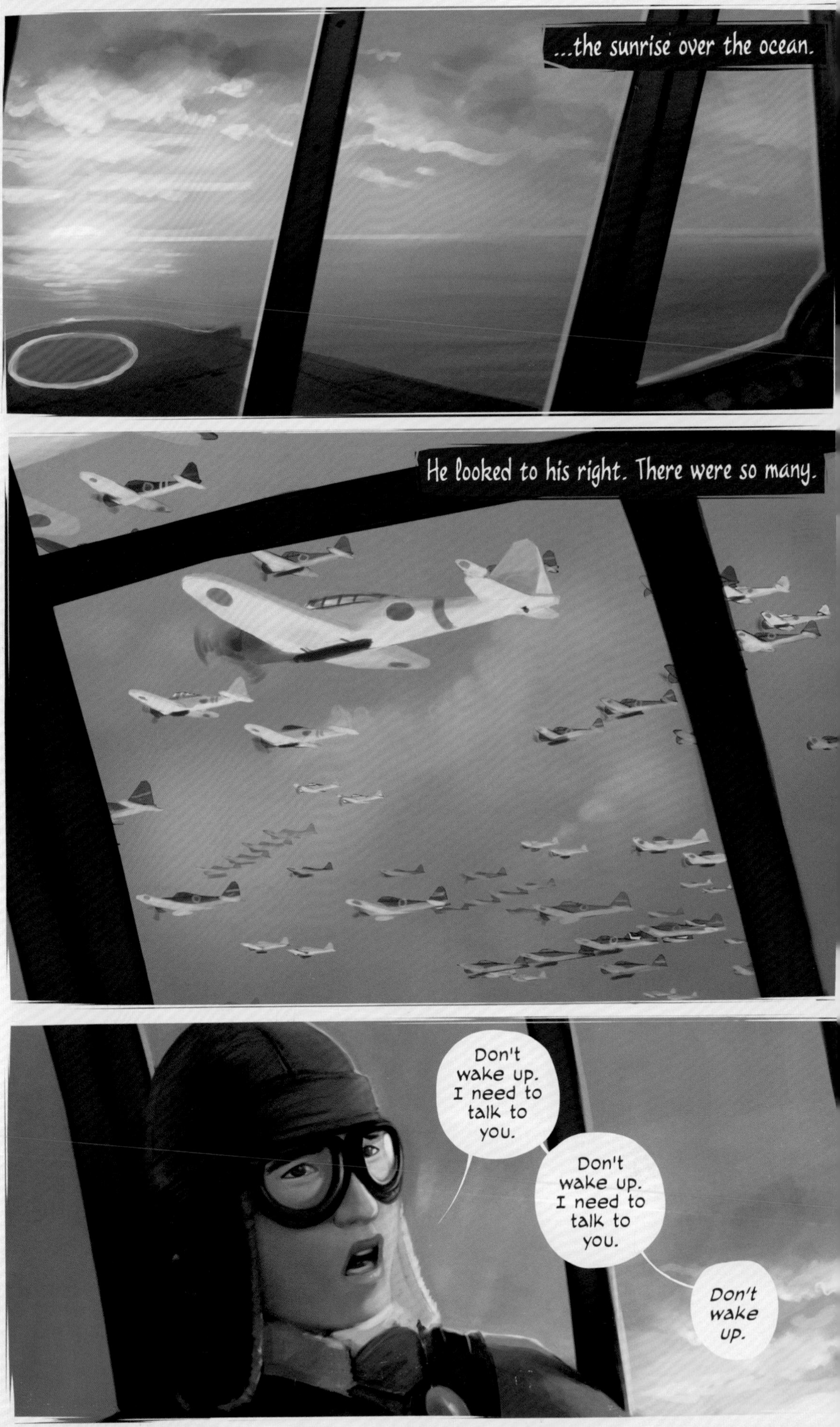
...the sunrise over the ocean.
He looked to his right. There were so many.
Don't wake up. I need to talk to you.
Don't wake up. I need to talk to you.
Don't wake up.

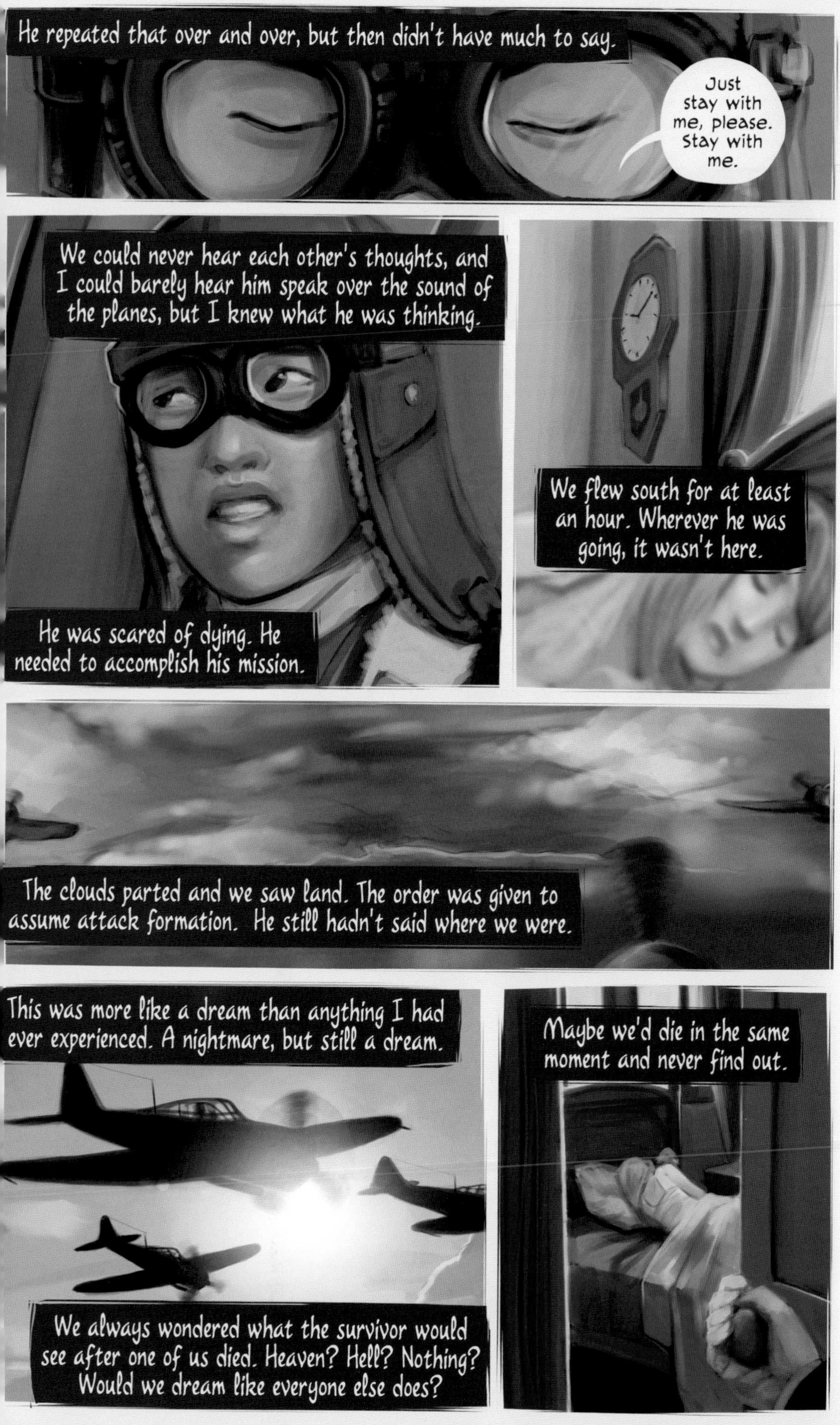
He repeated that over and over, but then didn't have much to say.
Just stay with me, please. Stay with me.
We could never hear each other's thoughts, and I could barely hear him speak over the sound of the planes, but I knew what he was thinking.
He was scared of dying. He needed to accomplish his mission.
We flew south for at least an hour. Wherever he was going, it wasn't here.
The clouds parted and we saw land. The order was given to assume attack formation. He still hadn't said where we were.
This was more like a dream than anything I had ever experienced. A nightmare, but still a dream.
We always wondered what the survivor would see after one of us died. Heaven? Hell? Nothing? Would we dream like everyone else does?
Maybe we'd die in the same moment and never find out.

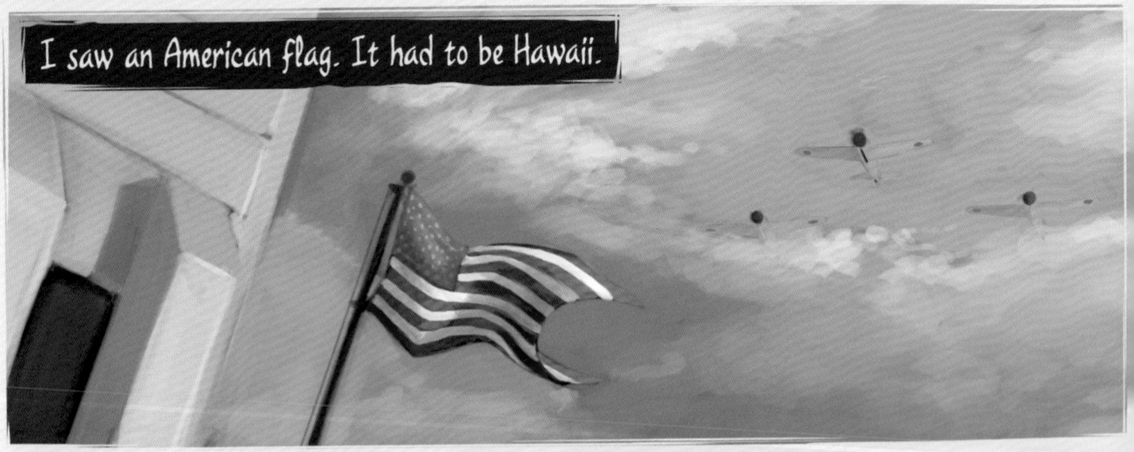
I saw an American flag. It had to be Hawaii.
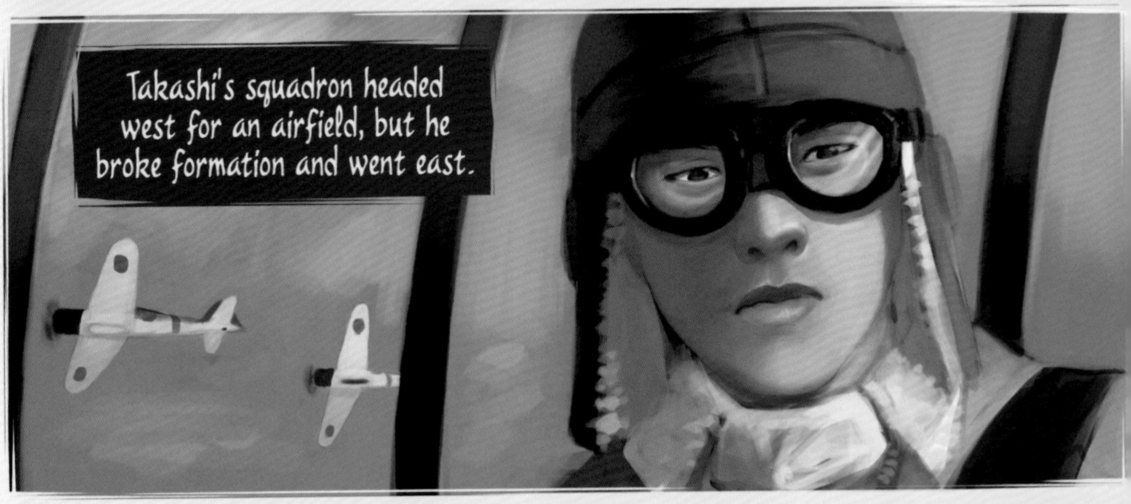
Takashi's squadron headed west for an airfield, but he broke formation and went east.
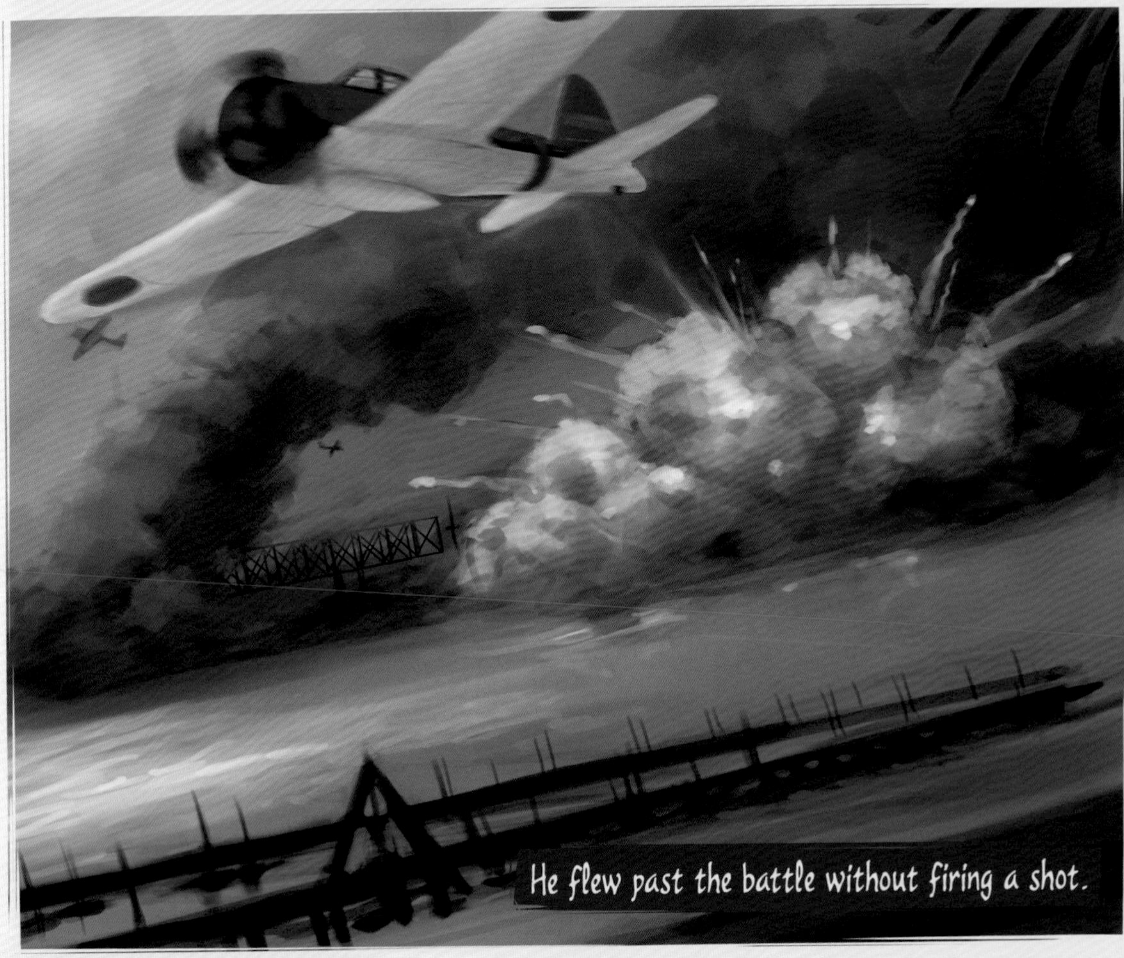
He flew past the battle without firing a shot.

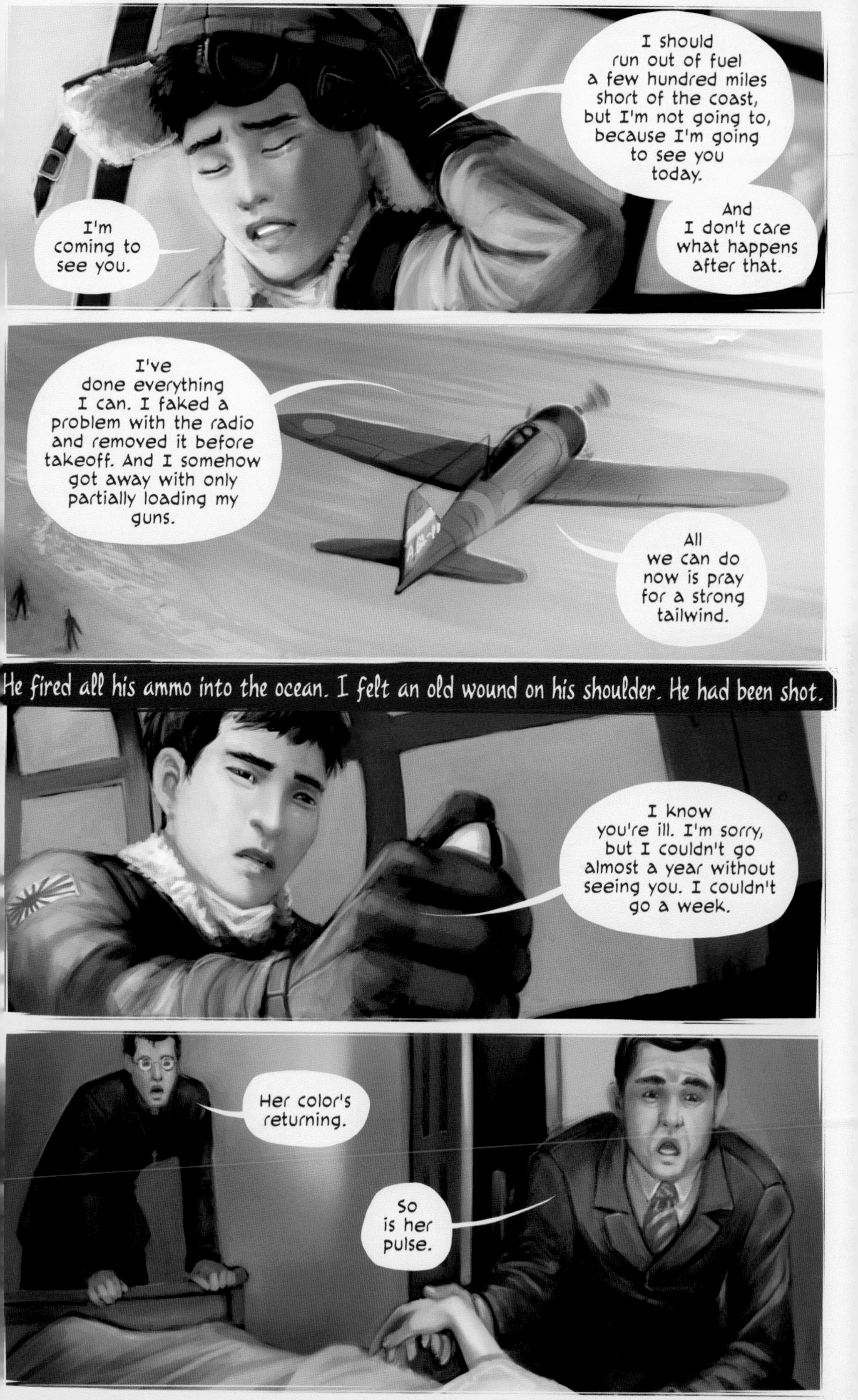
I'm coming to see you.
I should run out of fuel a few hundred miles short of the coast, but I'm not going to, because I'm going to see you today.
And I don't care what happens after that.
I've done everything I can. I faked a problem with the radio and removed it before takeoff. And I somehow got away with only partially loading my guns.
All we can do now is pray for a strong tailwind.
He fired all his ammo into the ocean. I felt an old wound on his shoulder. He had been shot.
I know you're ill. I'm sorry, but I couldn't go almost a year without seeing you. I couldn't go a week.
Her color's returning.
So is her pulse.

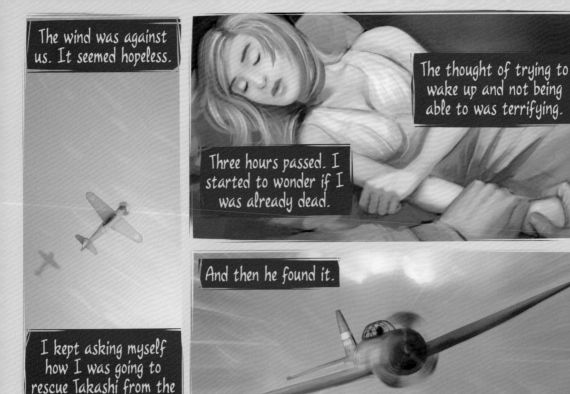

The wind was against us. It seemed hopeless.

The thought of trying to wake up and not being able to was terrifying.

Three hours passed. I started to wonder if I was already dead.

I kept asking myself how I was going to rescue Takashi from the ocean, and how I was going to live long enough to at least see him one time if he survived.

And then he found it.

We climbed to thirty thousand feet and the world changed. The strongest winds we've ever felt, right on our tail. It was like God was blowing him towards me.

We saw land the moment we ran out of fuel.

Don't worry. I can glide at least fifty miles from this height. Now I just need to find you.

Visibility was low. I had to wake up.

Dad.

We need to set fire to the trees around the lake. Now.

I'll do it.

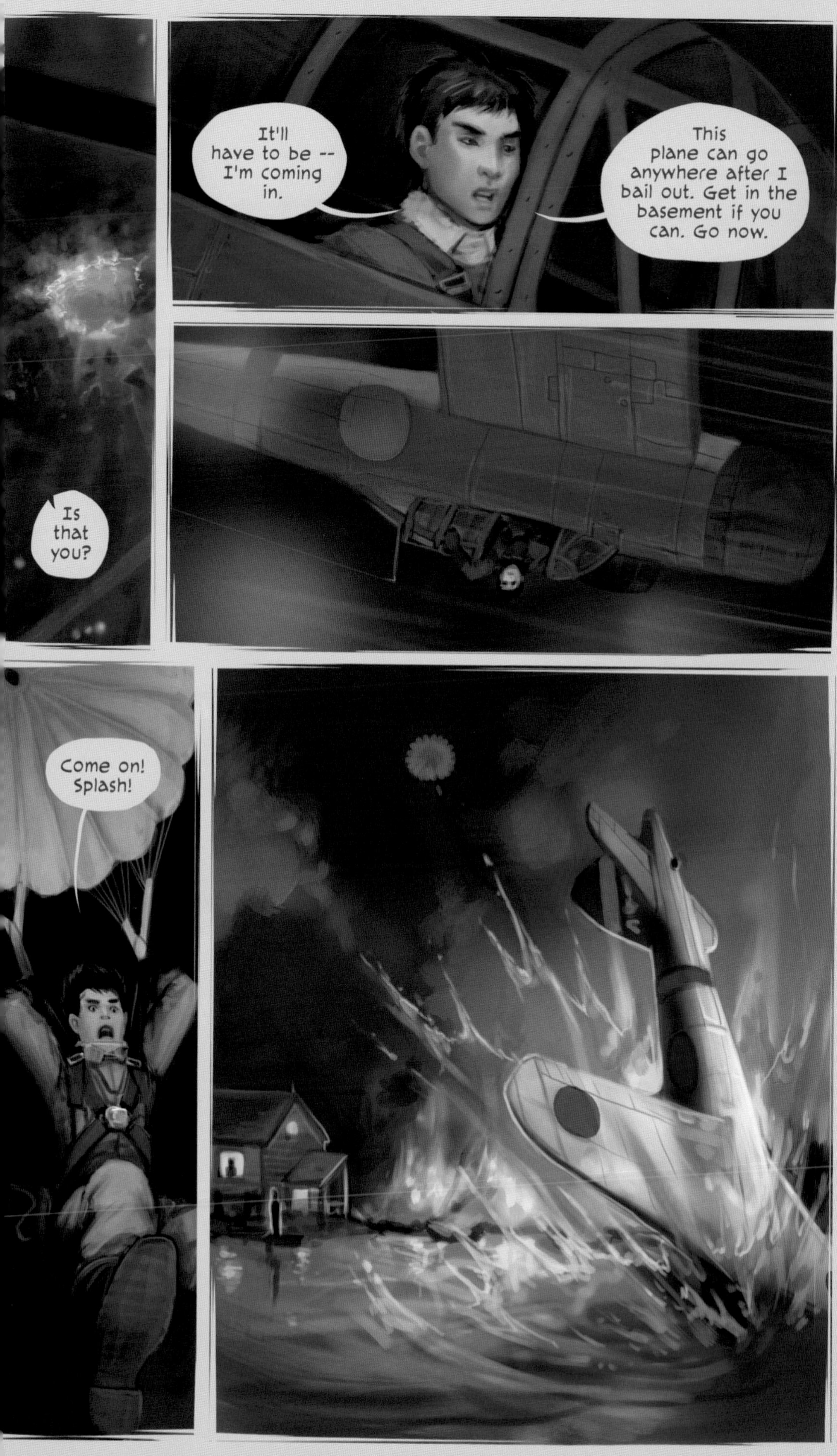
Is that you?
It'll have to be -- I'm coming in.
This plane can go anywhere after I bail out. Get in the basement if you can. Go now.
Come on! Splash!

I opened my eyes, jumped out of bed...

Elanor!

...flew down the stairs, burst through the door, and there he was.

Takashi!

The flames were drawing him in...

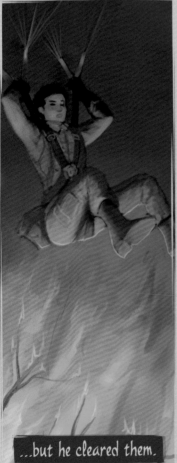

...but he cleared them.

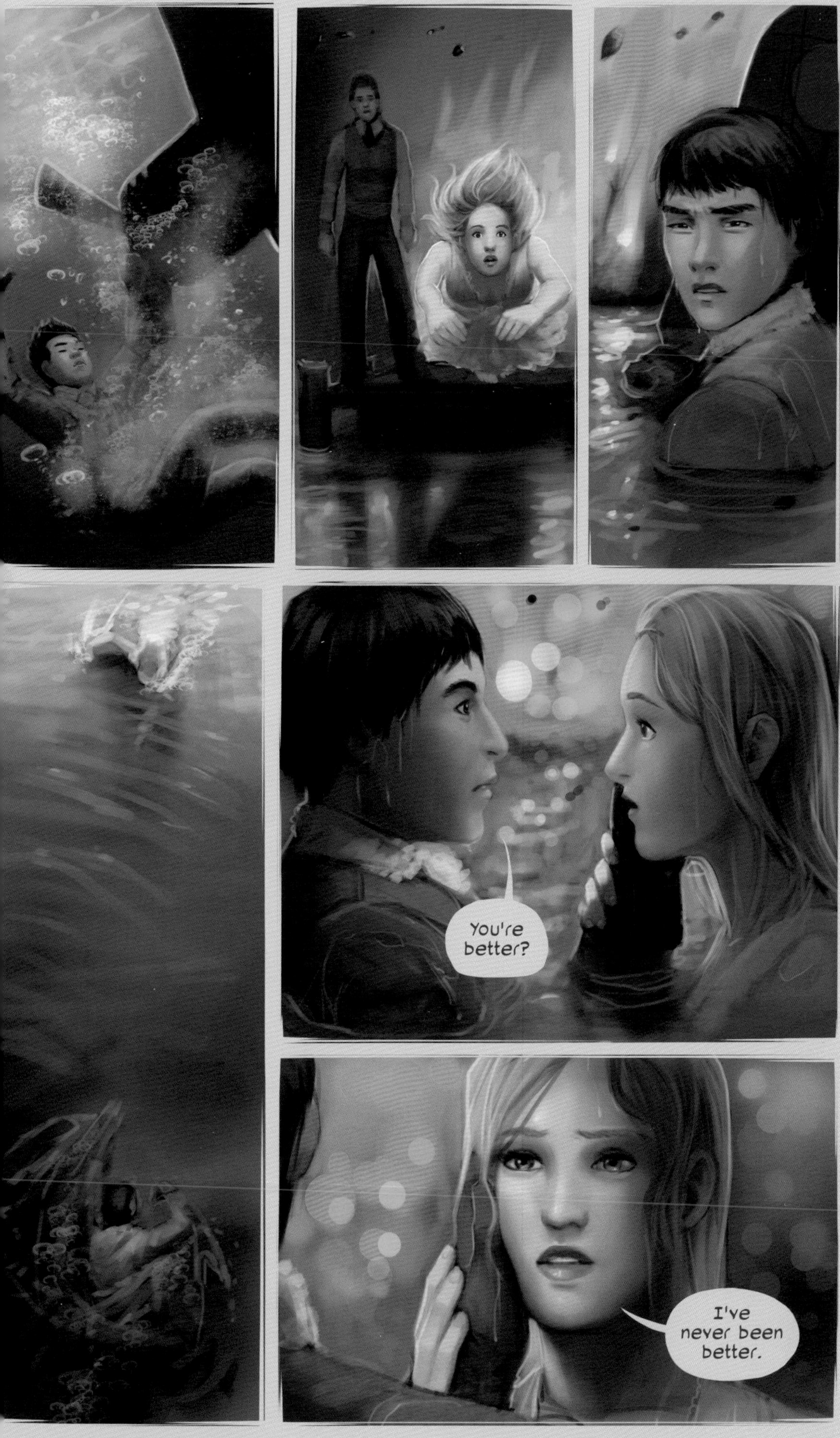
You're better?
I've never been better.

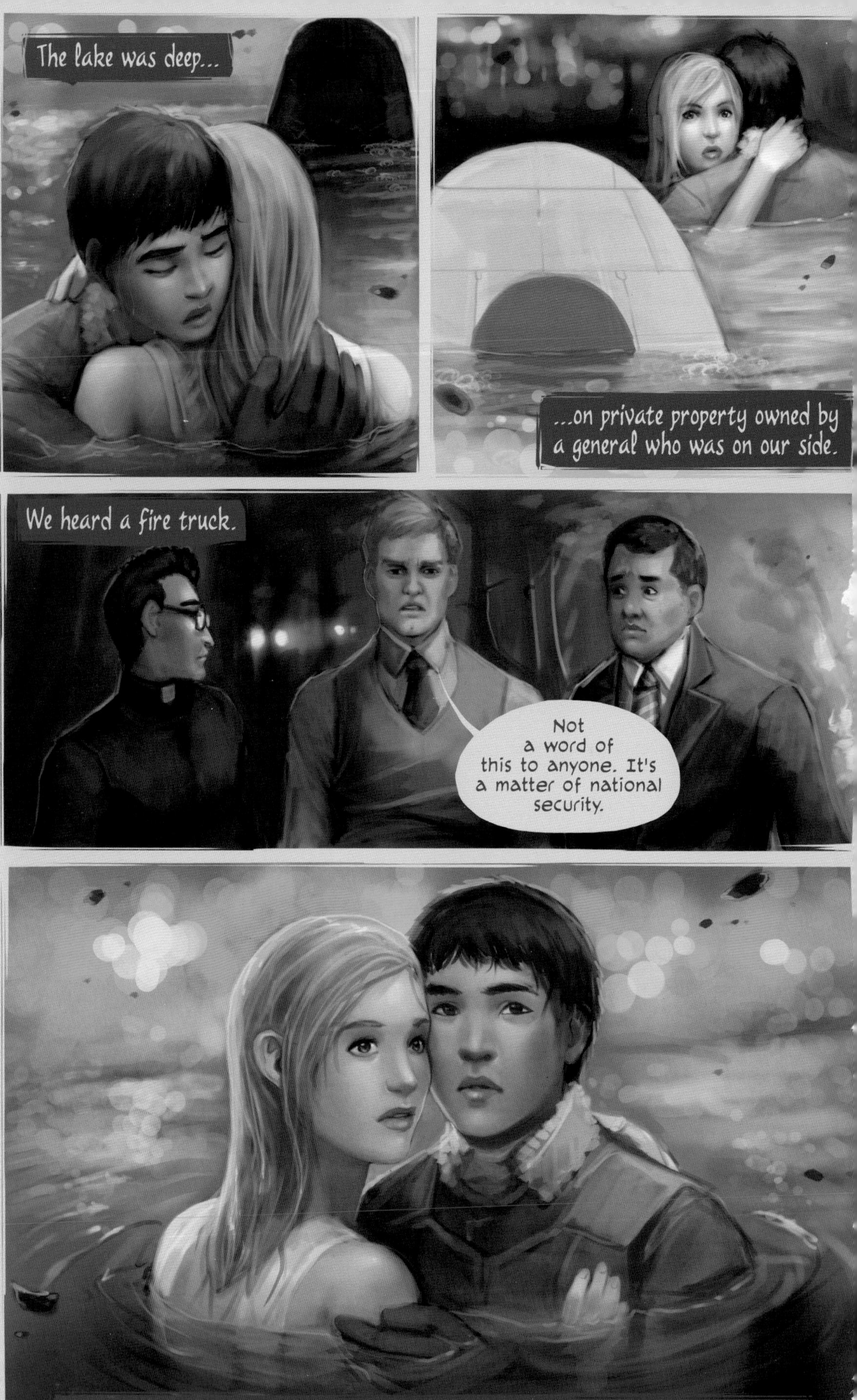
The lake was deep...
...on private property owned by a general who was on our side.
We heard a fire truck.
Not a word of this to anyone. It's a matter of national security.
We had finally met, and it was time to start caring about what happened next.